MONOMANIA
ELTON SKELTER

©2023 Elton Skelter

Elton Skelter

Monomania

Edited by Brett Mitchell Kent
Cover Design by Elton Skelter
Interior Design by God Plutonium (god94.com)
Published by Elton Skelter
Copyright 2023 Elton Skelter

License Notes
Thank you for downloading this book. This book remains the copyrighted property of the author, and may not be reproduced, copied and distributed for commercial or non-commercial purposes. If you enjoyed this book, please encourage your friends to purchase and download their own copy, where they can also discover other works by this author.

Thank you for your support.

Content Warnings:
This book contains, but is not limited to, the following triggering content. Reader discretion is advised: Gore, Abuse, Body Horror, Adult Language, Assault, Homophobia, Suicide and Suicidal Suggestion/Ideation, Substance Abuse, Murder, Revenge, Violence, Clowns, and LGBTQIA+ representation.

Elton Skelter

WHAT PEOPLE ARE SAYING

"Monomania is a riveting story that follows unforgettable final-girl characters through a deadly, suspense-filled weekend. I could not put this novella down until the bloody satisfying conclusion."

-Michelle Tang, Author

"Skelter delivers a tale that provides a human, realistic response to how one copes after experiencing a traumatic event such as mass murder spree. Surviving is one thing, but living after the fact is the challenge for this ensemble of characters.

Our final boy shows the harsh depths of dealing with pain, loss and guilt in the aftermath of their ordeal. Now, victim to his own emotions, the only way to overcome what happened is to go back to where it all began.

A fitting tribute to the slasher genre, and a fitting commentary on the modern fixation with true crime."

-Leeroy Cross James, Author of 'Camp Silver Oaks'

Elton Skelter

In American English

(ˌmanoʊˈmeɪniə)
NOUN

1. an excessive interest in or enthusiasm for some one thing; craze
2. a mental disorder characterized by irrational preoccupation with one subject

Elton Skelter

Monomania

--- THE NEWS, FOR YOU ---

HOUSTON TELEGRAPH

Tuesday   3 November 2009

LOCAL ANCHORWOMAN WINS BIG AT THE TEXAS BROADCAST NEWS AWARDS, FOURTH YEAR IN A ROW.

Since 2002, Texas native and broadcasting superstar, Rayna McCleod, has dominated the screens at Texas Central 103, a state-wide news channel dedicated to the latest in current events. McCleod, 35, two-time Peabody Award nominee and veteran of the airwaves, has become the unofficial face of the Lone Star State's news, covering everything from natural disaster, economic turmoil and international relations. In 2005, McCleod won the KUTX Broadcast News Award for her coverage of the Texas City Refinery explosion that killed 15 workers. Her tasteful and compassionate on-screen presence as well her cool tone and forward fashion has made her a popular figure in the cultural zeitgeist.

This year, for her impressive investigative acumen surrounding the corruption in the San Antonio Public School District, McCleod has yet again garnered the prestigious award, and has become the only female anchor in Texas history to receive the award in four consecutive ceremonies.

McCleod will be honored in the ceremony gathering in Houston in early 2010. More information to follow.

WIFE OF CONVICT FOUND DEAD, AGED 42

Tragedy struck outside of Dallas today when 42-year-old Kelly Michaelson took her own life at her private residence. This comes on the heels of the public scandal surrounding her husband, Leland Michaelson, who was one of the many teachers accused of corruption and bribery across the State's public school district.

This story broke early this year and led to a state-wide hunt for corruption and failing at the hand of educators in all levels of education, resulting in 27 prosecutions and 14 prison sentences based on severity.

Michaelson, 45, took his own life following the allegations. His widow was unable to cope with the loss, survived by a 16-year-old daughter, Elaine. Though the record is sealed, it is known that the child was taken into the foster care… *continued on page 7.*

Elton Skelter

CHAPTER 1

Elliot Hardy takes a swig of neat Maker's and listens to the ice clink against the side of the glass. It's 11.37am, but it's five o'clock somewhere and he hasn't slept in four days, so technically it's still Saturday night. The room reeks of stale marijuana and a saccharine combination of alcohol-laced sweat and Cheeto dust. An indent in the couch proves Elliot hasn't moved for days. The cushions are starting to stain an acrid-bile color beneath him. He suspects, if he knelt down to sniff them, he'd have to replace the whole damn couch. Alex Trebek's voice asks, too loudly with the TV speakers turned to max, "The smallest of the Great Lakes, it has a surface area of about 7,500 square miles."

"Michigan," Elliot slurs.

The answer is Ontario.

Trebek asks, "This band's 'Monster' album included 'Crush with Eyeliner'-"

Elliot yells, "Smashing Pumpkins!" Wrong again. It's

R.E.M, he hears, a second later.

He fishes a soft Cheeto from down the side of the couch cushion and tosses it at the screen, commiserates the failure with another three fingers of Marker's Mark. The ice has dissolved into nothing and too drunk and too idle, he forgoes the luxury of fresh ice for a room temperature libation.

An eerie, metallic screech from outside sounds in a hush between questions, the noise of the tiny, rusty flag of the mailbox being raised skyward against its wishes. Elliot wants to go to the curb side, but his legs won't support the journey, so he opts to leave the offerings in their weathered tin coffin. Teddy can pick them up on his way in.

Fuck, he thinks. *Teddy.*

The clock on the wall has lurched forward an hour in an instant and taunts him with its spry hands and working cogs. Theodor "Teddy" Meeker, the boyfriend who seems to love him despite everything he is but who is not so in love he'd tolerate this version of Elliot on too many occasions, is nearing the house by the second.

With a groan, Elliot lifts himself off the couch, scrambles to his feet, and shakes his head, a bad move that elicits nothing but the urge to purge the near half-bottle of bourbon he's consumed in the last hour. He rubs the sleep from his eyes, stinging them with the lingering liquor on his fingertips and heads for the stairs, his steps leaden and lazy and fighting him every step of the way.

Alex Trebek asks, "The sole survivor of the 2013 Frat House Massacre at Whitfield University."

Elliot quickens his pace up the stairs and closes the bathroom door behind him before he can hear his name

Monomania

being spoken in response.

By the time Teddy arrives, flustered, in a herringbone suit two sizes too big for him and looks like it's seen better days, the house no longer smells like a burnout's cavern. The jacket is a hand-me-down from his father's closet, a man who passed years before and that Teddy speaks about only in the abstract.

A rich roast pot of coffee burns fresh and has filled the lounge with the scent of a Costa Rican deep blend. Elliot showered and dressed and flipped the rancid couch cushions over and picked up all the discarded bottles, chips, and general debris from around the living space. To top it all off, his socks match, his collar is buttoned, and his breath tastes like the forced effort of trying to cover up several days of booze with a quick brush and an alcohol mouthwash. It's the best he could do in a pinch, but he's proud of himself, nonetheless. It's the small things.

Teddy lets himself in with the spare key Elliot had cut for him the week they started dating for the simple reason of him not wanting to get up to answer the door ever, and his shoulders are hunched and draped with string grocery bags spilling a cornucopia of fresh produce. There are eggplants and zucchini and bell peppers, and some weird green things Elliot has never seen before. He smiles at the offering, leans in for a quick kiss and registers this dietary offering as a very clear red flag. *This man*, he thinks, *is a monster*.

Once he has divested himself of the organic produce

in the heaped bags, Teddy shucks clumsily out of his jacket, his solid frame much more obvious and exposed in the tight-fitting button-down beneath. He clears his glasses of steam and the gentle glint of sweat from his trek and then pulls the mail from the side of one of the produce bags. Watching him, Elliot's heart starts to flutter, which was something he never thought he would feel again. Something about the man has him in a certain way he can't explain. As he takes the mail from Teddy's hand, he draws him in by the waist, luxuriating in the look, the feel of the solid man in his arms, and kisses him deeply. Teddy is thrown by the display, but leans into it, melting into the kiss with equal abandon, a smile forming on his lips that Elliot simply swallows with his own. Hands explore, heat rises, and Elliot pushes Teddy backwards slowly until his back is prone against the front door, Teddy's arms lifting and wrapping around his neck as he pulls the man close and deepens the connection. Elliot runs his hands the length of Teddy, knotting his fists around the tight fabric of his shirt, before settling his palms against the wooden door.

As if pathological, he finds himself sweeping the door for the locks, turning them one by one, ensuring they are secure. Teddy knows to do this as he enters and exits the house. The act is inconsequential, yet every fiber of Elliot's being screams for him to check as soon as it enters his mind. His kisses become absent, the mood flatlines, and Teddy pulls back, realizes the change in the heat and gives a small, almost imperceptible sign and slides out from where he is pinned between Elliot and the door.

"I'm sorry," Elliot says quietly, but still checks the locks. There are four in total, including a draw bolt that only gets fastened when he is secure inside the house, and a foot-activated deadbolt at the bottom of the door. Once everything is locked, he turns back to his partner and watches him skulk the small distance back to the kitchen island and start unpacking the produce from the hemp bags.

"It's fine," Teddy replies, not meeting his gaze when he finally tries to connect. "I know you can't help it."

The Clonazepam-Xanax-Prozac cocktail that has leveled out his various illnesses and disorders makes intimacy a rare commodity, coupled with the continuous stream of high-volume liquor consumed, and Elliot is all but impotent most days. Their relationship was never founded on sexual desire, though Elliot is the first to admit that it exists, and their sex life, when acted upon, has been good for the most part. Teddy never complains, and that is yet another reason Elliot loves him. Or another red flag?

He fights the desire to try and assuage Teddy and focuses on the letters strewn from the bag on the marble countertop. He gathers them up, seven in total, and tears each one open haphazardly, sheets of utility papers laden with red emerge like so much bloodshed. The electricity bill has a 30-day warning, the credit card he was using to pay the housing association has been declined. The circular payment method he devised to ensure everything was paid with credit from another source is now swallowing its tail.

Teddy chances a look back as he hoists the last of the produce into the crisper.

With a furrowed brow, Elliot regards the mess of mismatched puzzle pieces laid out on the scraps of paper. There is no way to plug something so discordant and out of control back together in a way that will render it fit for purpose. The money he makes writing has not been as healthy the past years and things have slipped. People were less enthusiastic to pay for the privilege or luxury of outside content creators and he had had little by way of high-paying work that allowed him to remain inside, safe in the bubble he created in the little house where his nightmares subside.

Teddy walks around the island, places a gentle hand on his shoulder and looks down at the mess. "If you need..." he begins.

Elliot raises a hand to shush him, to halt a conversation they have had many times before. As a professor at the local community college, Teddy is doing okay for himself. He has savings, he owns his car outright, the college gives him a subsidy on living expenses, and he is frugal almost to the point of seeming miserly. He has the money, Elliot knows, but it seems a step too far to acquiesce and take a handout from a man he can't even kiss without worry the locks of his front door like some agoraphobic maniac.

"You know I love your generosity, but it's my mess and I will be the one to clean it up." The words sound forceful enough to be honest, but they are tinged with regret, one that tastes like copper pennies and disbelief. How is he going to make this right?

The final envelope on the counter is smaller than the rest. Of thicker quality paper, his address is printed on the front in typewritten letters, like a wedding invitation or a gift card. Teddy backs off as he opens the small envelope, more careful than he was before, to save shredding the fine stationery.

It stares back at him, dawning on vacant eyes.

The invitation is for a trip back in time; a chance to unpick the past once and for all; a no holds barred interview about the night that changed everything, conducted by a national news crew with a viewership in the millions.

It is in the ruins of the old fraternity house, long since condemned and abandoned, the way he always felt it should be.

Cold sweat beads at his forehead as he feels the color drain from his face.

"El?" Teddy asks, concerned.

The stipend is fifteen thousand dollars, for one visit back to the place that has only existed in his mind's eye for a decade.

There is no way he can accept.

But there is no way he can refuse.

He looks again at the figure scrawled neatly in the offer.

Fifteen thousand dollars for a two-day long interview, all expenses paid, and the chance that it might finally jog loose that long stretch of repressed memory.

Elliot inhales sharply, resolved, and agrees to return to his own personal hell.

To try to know, once and for all, what happened that night.

The night he survived.

Elton Skelter

CHAPTER 11

In the time it takes him to sober up, Elliot is ready to start drinking again. Teddy gave him the pep-talk he knew was coming, enough to assuage the terror but not persuasive enough to wipe it out completely. The next morning Teddy squeezes his hand and gives him the comfort smile that makes him at once both warm and fuzzy and furious at the condescension, then leaves. With the door closed, it's straight to the freezer for the backup bottle of vodka hidden behind the ice pops and the burnt chicken breast fillets long over their expiration.

He forgoes the tumbler and takes a drag from the bottle, barely winces, immunity advanced and setting in. It still has that warming sensation going down, but the baseball bat to the head effect is a thing of the past.

Numbness sinks in, and he starts, against his better judgement, to allocate the finances to where he'd put them, loans and upgrades, new couch, and maybe a vacation. Maybe he could take Teddy somewhere nice or, maybe just leave him behind and head for the hills. It all sounds too appealing, but at what cost?

In the throes of recovery, it's easier to be more subjective. It's just a place, Whitfield. It's just the empty husk of a place he used to know. It's bricks and mortar and bad décor, but it holds no power. There are no bad guys hiding in crawlspaces, no knife-wielding psychos going room to room. The memories are all the power that's left of that period. And the memory, essentially, is lost to the annals of time.

His chest thuds, regardless.

The voice in his head is loud but reflex is a whole other beast, one he can't control. The vodka goes down smoother on the second draw.

He turns the invitation over and scans the words, the generous figure, the embossed script like it was pounded in with a retro typewriter. For the first time he sees it; a contact number. He kicks himself for not spotting it and dialing it up sooner, but the rush of the booze has given him the confidence he needs to do so.

There is no point in torturing himself, not until he has all the information.

Another swig for liquid courage and he dials the number on the landline, hears it ring three times before a clumsy hand fumbles the answer.

A soft voice answers, out of breath, gasps the details of some news station—Texas Central 103—or something of that ilk. "Can I help you?" the woman asks, still fighting the tightness in her chest.

Elliot feels it, too. The strain.

"Hi," he says, and his voice creaks. "My name is Elliot Hardy. I got a letter?" He can't think what else to say but the silence on the other end stretches too long.

"Oh my God," the woman says, finally finding her breath in the wake of over-exertion. "It's really you?"

"Last I checked," he jokes, making the woman laugh. Forced, over the top. Elliot is a lot of things but he's not funny. He could have been—perhaps—but in this life, funny is not an option.

"It's really, honestly, you? I've read everything about you! It was my idea to do this," She talks a mile a minute and it breaks the tension. Elliot can't think what he needs to ask now that he holds the handset in his sweating palm. *Why was he even calling?*

"Please, please, please...tell me you're gonna do it?" Her voice is liquid, saccharine under the weight of desperation. "I would simply *die*-" She catches herself, but she's already said it. People don't typically like to use that word around him. He doesn't particularly like it himself, bites his tongue until he tastes blood. "I'm so sorry," she says, mortified by his silence.

"It's fine," Elliot lies, but she knows it's not even through the phone, even from miles away, she knows.

"So, are you calling-"

"-To speak to Rayna McCleod, yeah." He stares down at the card dampening in his fist, sees Rayna's name staring back. She's not a TV personality, not one he's heard of. The smaller letters under her name read *Executive Producer – Current Events.*

"Rayna...right! Let me patch you through." The click of a button and it's hold music on the line, the kind you hear in elevators, the kind they pipe in at the mall to avoid copyright issues.

When she answers, Rayna McCleod sounds like the exhaust of a hand-me-down car, the type of twenty-a-day smoker that they use to make a point on bad shows, the type she no doubt has some hand in. "McCleod," she says, and it sounds more like a command than a greeting.

"Uh…Ms. McCleod…" he cringes. He has never called anyone *Ms.* in his entire life. "I got a card from you. An offer. Said to call?"

She harumphs down the line. "Who may I ask is calling?" It's not polite. She just sounds bored.

"My name is Elliot Hardy," he says, and he can almost hear the change in her expression despite not being able to see her face.

Rayna, now a different woman it seems, makes an inhuman happy sound, and Elliot can swear she slaps her thigh, Texas-style. "Elliot! Oh, it's so good to hear from you!"

Elliot rolls his eyes, letting the sugary sweetness of her pretense fill his ears like wax.

"So, here's the pitch," she says, undeterred.

For the next twenty minutes, all he can do is grunt in acknowledgement between riffed ideas and spun yarns, tall orders for short attention spans.

The thing that really gets him is that this is not his show. He's just one of a few, not a star but part of a group.

Rayna is calling them *survivors*.

Rayna is a ghoul.

Fifteen thousand dollars, he tells himself. *Fifteen thousand dollars.*

And honestly, if he admits it to himself, he'd do it for less. There's a trade-off here, for sure. He can be a puppet for a few days of shocked expressions and traumatized looks if it keeps the fridge stocked and his liver pickled.

He's so lost he doesn't realize she's stopped her pitch. "Elliot? What do you think?"

"About what?" he asks, dumbly, and winces.

"About the show, silly!" Her drawl accentuates in a playful way. He hates her, already.

Elliot could just not. He could hang up the phone and stay home, hunker down with Teddy and let the chips fall where they may.

But there's that voice in the back of his head: *fifteen thousand dollars, fifteen thousand dollars.*

"Make it $25k and you got yourself a deal," he finds himself saying, and the honey-drip of her voice dries up.

"Listen, kid, I had to fight for that fifteen, there's no way they are offering more. You're not even the most interesting guest we're seeing."

"But I'm the most well-known, right? And I'm the only one you're making go back to where it happened?"

Gotcha, he thinks in the space between her labored rage.

"Twenty-k, and that's as high as I'll go," she says after a minute. He taps his fingers on the counter, like he's thinking about it, like he's weighing up the options.

"Fine," he says, after a strenuous amount of pregnant silence.

Her façade has shattered, and she doesn't try to build it back up. "There's a ticket waiting for you at O'Hare for Saturday. Be on the plane on time." Elliot thinks she's going to hang up, but he can still hear the crunch of sprayed hair on office plastic, the jangle of a gaudy earring against the receiver. "I'll have my assistant call with all the details but *be on that plane.*"

He's going. He's really going. His gut starts to ache,

his hand instinctively reaching beyond the flat white card and to the perspiring vodka just within grasp.

"And Elliot?" she asks, this time waiting for his response.

"Yeah?"

"Don't fuck this up." The line goes dead, bottoms out as quickly as his gut. He pulls the bottle to his lips and takes a pull and it burns all the way down.

Saturday will come, he knows, too quickly to stave off. But come Monday, he'll be set for the rest of the year.

In the back of his mind, he wonders what else he'll end up bringing home.

Monomania

GENERAL INFORMATION		
Witness Name: Morris Gaudello, Campus Dean	**Witness Cell Phone:** +1 (713) 456-0092	**Witness Campus/Dept:** Whitfield University, Main Campus, Greek Row
Location of Incident: Phi Kappa Delta frat house	**Victim Name:** Elliot Hardy, 20, Male	**Date of Incident:** 07-26-2013
Criminal Department: Homicide	**Date of Witness Statement:** 07-27-2013	**Time Statement Taken:** 9.17am

STATEMENT

At approximately 11.38pm, Mr. Gaudello, the campus Dean of Admissions, was alerted by campus security of an incident at the Phi Kappa Delta house on Greek Row. An unidentified caller had reported the incident to the campus security team who then called the local authorities.

Mr. Gaudello, who lives on campus, was first to arrive on the scene. He states that when he arrived at the Phi Kappa Delta house, he saw one person sitting on the front steps of the property. This was 20-year old student Elliot Hardy, who was in shock, covered in blood and cuts and unresponsive to questioning.

Once ensuring the student was not likely to move, but that they had not sustained serious injury, Mr. Gaudello went into the property, fearing someone else was hurt.

He reports seeing blood upon entering, a trail of which led into the communal area, where he found the corpses of three students, who all were deceased.

He admits that after seeing this, his mind became foggy, and he forgets how he made it up the stairs to the second floor of the building. He does recall going door to door and locating the bodies of another seven slain students in their respective bedrooms, and in the final room he checked the body of faculty member Mr. Ethan Radkin, who was unrecognizable due to his injuries, save for his staff ID badge.

Mr. Gaudello stated that Mr. Radkin had no professional or personal links to the house and had no reason to be there at that hour and that his presence was alarming.

On further questioning, he admitted he heard rumors of this faculty member fraternizing with students, particularly young male students, and that the rumors had been ignored, put down to conjecture.

When asked about the mental state of the inhabitants of the fraternity, Mr. Gaudello stated that they were typical boys who liked to drink and party, pull pranks, but all of whom kept their grades up to standard to avoid removal from their fraternity. He did not recall any of the students being subject to disciplinary action of any kind.

He stated that the victims were not the only members of the fraternity, and the rest were likely absent due to studying, staying with their girlfriends or partying off campus. The fraternity had an additional 10 members whose families were being contacted by campus security.

When asked what he suspected had occurred that night, Mr. Gaudello was reticent to answer. After some probing, he admitted he wondered if the deceased faculty member had become inappropriate with one or more of the house and had perhaps targeted them for redemption or retribution, but said he felt that this was simply theory, and that the only way to truly know was to speak with Elliot Hardy, the only remaining member of the fraternity that had been there and had made it out alive.

We thanked Mr. Gaudello for his input and told him we would be in contact should we have more questions.

Interview terminated at 10.37am 07/27/2013

Statement taken by: Officer Kenneth Laudermilk, Houston PD.

Elton Skelter

CHAPTER III

Lana DeSteffano arranges her pills in the caddy, Monday through Sunday, the same way she does every week, when the call comes. She jumps with a yelp. It's been a long time since someone other than her therapist called, and even then, she usually calls through Zoom video. The ring of the cell sounds obscene in the muted silence of the dimly lit kitchen.

October for Lana is a nightmare. It's been forty-five years, give or take a week, and nothing ever gets better, and nothing ever gets easier. Not after what happened. She watches her cell ring until it gives up and pushes the call to answerphone. Only then does her heart start to beat at a normal pace again.

In this day and age, you need a cellphone. There's no getting around it. If she had her way, she would never so much as look at a telephone again. Every time she does, she can't help but conjure *that* night, the cop's voice on the line as he told her the call was coming from inside the house. She'd kill to never have experienced that, to never have to take or make a phone call, to go back and save her seventeen-year-old self from what would come.

As Halloween night creeps ever closer, Lana knows that it will only get worse; the tightness in her chest will grip closed like a vice, the paranoia, seeing things from the corner of her eye. She'll sleep with a gun beneath her pillow, like she always does, but through October, she'll keep it loaded. It's a wonder she hasn't blown her own head off playing it that way, but in a way she's been blessed in that respect.

But not in any other.

Lana tried to make it all okay, tried every therapy, every drug, every misguided vice that pulled her in and out of her trauma, and in the end nothing had really worked.

At least now she could go outside, that alone had taken years to accomplish. She'd made the journey step by step, each day walking a little further beyond her door, until one day, she could just be outside, and not feel the need to run home and bolt the doors, set the alarm, and crawl under her sheets. But there's a lot that goes with that, including a carefully planned drug regime and an obscene amount of breathing exercises.

She finishes pocketing the last of Sunday's pills into their slot and must force the lid down on the caddy to close it. Her cell phone rings again, same sound, same reaction. This time, she looks at the screen, sees it's an unknown number and skips the call to voicemail. This time, after a few minutes, it chimes for a voicemail. She doesn't jump to listen, doesn't rush the process at all. Instead, she turns to the cupboard and starts to rifle through a selection of herbal teas, all organized by flavor profile and homeopathic attribute. She pulls a pack of blackberry-mint from the cupboard and closes the door, then sets to preparing it, lowering the bag into a cup of cold water and draping the string over the rim, microwaving the cup until the water turns molten and steam billows off the surface of the purpling liquid.

When Lana sips the tea, she burns her lips and tongue. "Aw, fuck," she mutters before placing the cup down on the counter beside the pill caddy. She breathes in deeply through her nose, holds the breath for a count of five and then exhales slowly through her mouth, feeling the tension in her shoulders unwind. Another breath and her back starts to unknot. Another and she's back to normal.

As normal as she can, at least.

She sets the caddy at a perfect 45-degree angle against the cup. All things in their place, everything lined up perfectly. Predictable, manufactured control, the only kind she will accept. That, too, is another holdover from the night her life nearly ended, the night he came for her.

She checks the lock on the back door, unlocks it and locks it again five times until the routine is complete, until the side of her created in 1978 is sated, convinced the small ceremony is enough to ensure her safety. She sets the alarm with the six-digit code.

10-31-78.

She has never managed to escape the significance, like that night was the night she was truly born, not the girl who clawed and fought to hang onto life, but the girl that was left over when the night was through. The one holding on by only the tips of bloodied fingers, nails lifted and wrecked from their beds. *That* girl was the only one left standing when the dust settled.

She takes her steaming teacup to the couch, folds her legs beneath her and only then allows herself to start scrolling through her cell.

Again, she chooses to ignore the voicemail and opens up the new email.

All the tension returns to her shoulders as she reads the name: Rayna McCleod.

The woman was a vulture. For the past five years, at the same time every year, she had been hounding Lana for an interview, a tell-all story that she had always refused to give. What more was there to say? And how, after so many years could she show everyone how little progress she had made?

She clicks the email and reads, and tension makes way to anger.

Lana,

It's that time of year again, the time I ask you if you'd be willing to share your story. I know in the past we haven't always been able to forge ahead with a plan that suits us both, but I think I've found something that might put all your fears to rest.

I'm calling it "the survivor special".

Lana reads on, blood boiling at the audacity until she sees the figure at the foot of the email. They had never discussed payment before, but this…well, this was something else.

For your troubles and for the privilege of sharing your story with all those other survivors who are fighting their battles alone, the studio is willing to pay $25k and include all expenses for the trip.

$25k would go a long way to ensuring her comfort,

Monomania

that is for sure.

But it doesn't change anything. She still has nothing left to say.

Lana reads and re-reads the email until she can quote it verbatim, until it is the only thing left in her head. Her boiling blood settles to a simmer, the tension less tense than before.

Twenty-five-thousand dollars? She will sleep on it, but she makes no mistake that the offer has piqued her interest. Enough to go back to that terrible night for one last time?

She'll wait until morning to decide, but she already knows the answer.

Elton Skelter

Monomania

POLICE REPORT

Case No: _____347802933_____   Date: _____10-31-1978_____

Reporting Officer: __Lt. Sam Hannahford, ISPC__   Prepared By: __Sherilyn Brand, ISPD__

Incident: _____Mass murder, unknown assailant, single survivor_____

On the night of October 31st, 1978, Halloween Night, the small community of Pleasance Summit, Illinois, was visited upon by a single killer. The final remaining victim managed to fight her way to freedom before chasing away a masked assailant, male, approximately 6 feet tall. The mask was pure white with attached hair. He was dressed in blue, with work boots on his feet.

The victim's name is Lana DeSteffano, aged 17, a local girl, who presented at the station accompanied by officers. She had wounds on her arm, neck and leg. None of her injuries were life-threatening.

Miss DeSteffano was interviewed in attendance with her mother, Anika DeSteffano, and a female officer, Officer Sherilyn Brand.

Miss DeSteffano was visibly shaken, trembling with fear and crying throughout the interview. She and her mother gave express permission for the interview to be conducted before she was taken to Pleasance Summit General for medical examination. Her wounds had been temporarily covered with bandages by EMTs on site at the final location of the incident.

Miss DeSteffano recounted that she had been hired to care for two children on the night in question and had been alone at the residence at the time of the attack, save for the children, one boy and one girl, who had been asleep when she had arrived. Upon settling down to watch a movie, she stated that the house's telephone had begun to ring, and she had answered it immediately so as not to startle the children awake. She stated there was nobody speaking on the other end of the line, and she suspected it was a friend playing a Halloween prank. She hung up the phone and was startled by the police sirens driving past the residence (this pertains to cases 347802930, 347802931 and 347802932).

At this point in the evening, she was unaware of the other incidents which had occurred in the vicinity and continued to watch her movie.

At around 10pm, the telephone rang again, and this time she reports that a man with a graveled voice spoke to her, asking if she had checked on the children. She thought this odd but went to check on them and found them both asleep.

When she descended the stairs, the front door of the property was ajar and she realized that something was wrong, as she had made a point to lock the door herself earlier in the evening. She stated that she locked the door again and slowly made her way through the house, checking for anything amiss.

*The phone began to ring again, and she answered to same the man, who warned her to ...**continued overleaf***

Elton Skelter

CHAPTER IV

Elliot doesn't remember the day leading up to the trip, how he packed a bag haphazardly, how he motivated himself to remember everything he might need. He doesn't remember the repeat conversations with Rayna's assistant, the details about flight times and boarding passes, the instructions about the driver who would meet him at George Bush Intercontinental to drive him back to the campus. He represses it all, and somehow, by some miracle of autopilot or muscle memory, he readies himself for a trip backwards in time.

On Saturday morning, Elliot makes toast and scrambled eggs he can't stomach to eat, drinks four cups of coffee, and checks multiple times that he has packed all his meds, his cell charger, and enough cash should he need it. He plans to pick up two large bottles of liquor from the airport store and hopes it will be enough to last him through the weekend.

At eleven, the Uber he forgets he ordered arrives to

take him to O'Hare. While the cab idles on the curb outside, he checks his cell, finds a message from Teddy.

You got this. I believe in you. T x

The words of encouragement do nothing to assuage the tornado of caffeinated mania rupturing inside of him. He lets himself out of the house, locks the door, once, twice, again and again, follows the ritual until he's satisfied that he has safeguarded the house in some supernatural way.

The sun in the sky is too bright, hurts his eyes so he must squint against the brightness. He can't remember the last time he left the house, let alone the state. He stops with his hand on the car door, lets his eyes adjust to the light before opening it and climbing inside.

"All set, Mr. Hardy?" the driver asks. Elliot feigns a smile, nods his head. The rumble of the old engine vibrates through him as they peel away from the house.

He knows it's just his mind, but he wonders if he left the stove on, if he really locked the door, if this were the one time that he left the faucets running in the upstairs bathroom.

But it's too late now. No turning back.

Instead, he focuses his mind on the driver, to what little of the man's face he can see in the rearview reflected back at him. His eyes are deep-set, dark as brown can go without crossing over into black. A scratchy beard coats the lower half of his jaw, never quite connecting with the patchy tufts of his moustache. His face looks kind, Elliot decides. But kindness means nothing. He's seen kind before and underneath it all, what's on the surface counts for shit.

He realizes how tight he's clutching his cell, loosens his grip and types a message back to Teddy.

Thank you. See you soon. Love you x

He hits send without a second thought, without thinking that in that brief communication, he told Teddy he loves him for the first time. It doesn't even register until the reply comes back, a harsh buzz in his clenched palm.

Love you too x

It's not enough to stave off the shakes that build in his irate legs, in his restless limbs. He is a live wire of raw, kinetic energy and the cab is a prison designed to keep him spinning off out of control.

With the addition of weekend traffic, the drive to O'Hare takes forty-five minutes.

He barely remembers any of them.

Elton Skelter

CHAPTER V

Remy Devereaux dodged the first punch but wasn't quick enough to move away from the second. It connects with his jaw with the force of a freight train and, the next thing he knows, he is face down in the dirt, cartoon birdies forming a crown around his head. He blames the booze, of course, but part of the distraction, part of the reason he's not fighting his best fight, is the thought of Rayna *fucking* McCleod's voice on the phone.

It had been years since he'd last heard it, years of blissful sobriety, his mind able to start to repair and mend from the trauma, and one call with her had undone it all. He climbs to his knees in the dirt, but a firm kick to his ribs leaves him winded, breathless, and back on the ground.

That feeling. The air refusing to fill his lungs. It takes him back.

Camp St. Agnes was a lifetime ago, but now even thinking the name smarted like hell. And with that feeling, the fear was not far behind. Fear for his life, fear of the ominous silhouette of a man stalking the lakeside, going cabin to cabin with the axe in his hands. The fear of who he had become to get out of there alive.

Admittedly, he'd thought of just hanging up the phone, but Rayna knew him well enough not to bury the lead.

"Ten thousand dollars," she'd started, and the pitch had been a success from there. He hated himself for being so desperate for cash that he would give in to a self-serving hack like Rayna, but cash is cash, and you can't live without it. Was living what he had been doing?

The man walks away from the fight, resolute that Remy is down and out, walks back to his friends and takes a bottle of beer from the hand of a young woman, swigs and gulps it down in one, throws the bottle to the ground, too close to where Remy lies, insult on injury.

At least she hadn't tried to sell him on the old pitch, the one that had been coming regularly for years: a return to the campgrounds to face his demons. Compared to that, this would be a cake walk. The day they took him from St. Agnes to the hospital, he had sworn to never set foot back in that place and he had kept that promise to himself. Twenty years had passed, and he hadn't let himself down in that respect.

In every other, he hadn't been so successful.

Rayna was cagey on the details, a university campus in Texas, some place where something happened years back, but she wouldn't tell him what. A quick Google search and it had become clearer. Another town, another teenage massacre. Same day, different weather.

Remy brushes the dirt from his knees and winches

at the raw skin on the palms of his hands, small bits of gravel and flecks of sawdust stick to the specks of rising blood there, but it doesn't faze him.

Ten grand for a couple of days auditing some other nightmare.

After the last twenty years, this won't hurt one bit. Smile for the cameras, cry if you can. He knows how this works.

But Rayna. If he could, he'd take a swing at her, knock her down a peg or two. Remy isn't violent by nature, but there are some things that speak to the beast in you. And since Camp St. Agnes, there's something dark hidden inside.

He thinks of Rayna, of the lost sobriety, of all those AA chips now rendered useless, when he climbs to his feet.

And he's thinking of her when he walks across the lot, pulls back his hand, and slams it into the back of the guy's head.

He tries not to smile as the man goes down, hard, unconscious, and out for the night. Guys like Remy, they don't stay down long. They have their battles, and sometimes they get the shit kicked out of them.

But they always get back up.

And they always get the last punch.

Elton Skelter

Monomania

Police Department Report

Case Number: 010004 **Date:** 08/05/2003

At the site of Camp St. Agnes, a summer camp for teens, on the eve of opening to the public, a series of violent murders were documented by the sole remaining survivor, 17-year-old Remy Devereaux of Concordia Parish, Louisiana. Full details of the attacks have not yet been gathered, but this is the preliminary record of the state of the victim at the time he was taken into custody.

Mr. Devereaux was found catatonic, unresponsive to stimulus and unable to answer questions. He was taken to be examined by medical professionals and then was removed to the psychiatric unit for observation and treatment.

We were unable to get any statement from the victim at this time.

Physical examination reveals defensive marks from a sharp blade on both hands and forearms, a head injury conducive with concussion and an injury to his right ankle.

Pupils were responsive, pain stimuli were positive, and the victim showed signs of auditory distress when confronted with loud noises. More information will be gathered when it is appropriate to do so.

The victim is considered a risk to himself and has been placed on minimum psychiatric hold of 72-hour. Physical evidence at the scene is indicative of a mortal engagement with a deranged individual (deceased) who is yet to be identified. Camp St. Agnes will remain closed until investigation complete.

Reporting Officer: Patrolman Augustus C Haverland **Date:** 5th Aug 2003

Notary/Law Enforcement Officer: Glenis Mordeckai, county notary

Supervisor Approval: Chief Renault Radimski **Date:** 6th August 2003

Elton Skelter

CHAPTER VI

Rayna kicks her feet up on the desk, leans back in the creaking leather chair and smiles, cigarette smoke billowing from the tip of a Lucky Strike. She shouldn't smoke in the office, but after this deal, she's all but indispensable. The camera crew and the site manager both had been working around the clock to ensure the place was ready, and on the small monitors mounted against the crowded wall of her office, she had been able to sit back and watch it all unfurl.

Seeing it come to life is a matter of extreme pride for her. It was a stroke of genius to start with, compounded by the infusion of the financial beneficiaries who came forward to support the livestream.

This is the closest thing to a convention of victims the world will ever get. And she'll be right there on the front lines, asking the questions, watching as these poor downtrodden fucks spill their darkest secrets, mourn the loss of their innocence. She'll be the face of the whole thing, with a support of characters from across the decades, all different but all bound together.

Tragedy makes vultures of us all.

She stubs the cigarette out on the desk while looking upward at one of the newer monitors, top corridor. The house has been returned to former glory, not that it was ever much to write home about. A lick of paint, some spackle and stucco and it's like going back in time, or at least from what she can tell of the photographs. She's stuck prefab over decay, and though the smell of wet paint will still be pungent come the arrival, it's not exactly an olfactory attraction. It'll capture perfectly for television and that's really all that matters.

She's not likely to win any popularity contests with the cut corners, but Rayna isn't in the business of making friends.

This is showbiz, baby.

"Anya, will you come in here?" she asks in the intercom, and a crackle of static rings back in answer.

Less than a minute later, the mousey assistant is all but falling through the office door. She rights herself before she topples onto the mildewy carpet. Wrinkles her nose at the cigarette stench. "Rayna?" she asks, expectantly, eyes wide like prey caught in the crosshairs of the hunters' barrels.

"Have we heard back from everyone?" Rayna asks, not taking her eyes off the screens for a second longer. She pulls another smoke blindly from the packet on the desk and lights it without looking.

"Uh, yes, Rayna. We've had confirmation from all eight of the…" She can't finish the thought or find the word she needs to describe everyone she's been talking to the last week. *Victims* seems too harsh. *Survivors* too patronizing. "Guests," she settles on. "All are set to arrive on Saturday afternoon, just before dinner. The restaurant is booked for 6pm, and the rooms are all ready, microphones live, and cameras will be set within the hour."

The microphones, they were a sticking point. The investors wanted them, but legal had a thing or two to say, particularly when Rayna suggested they not tell the participants about them. Audio recorded is off bounds for public use outside of the common areas, and the rooms are to remain camera free. Rayna, despite her natural pessimism, is counting on these freaks to make use of the confessional cameras, for those close-ups of broken faces and faraway glances.

It'll all come out in the wash.

What she needs is the raw footage, the things they might not want to say in front of a camera man, in front of the wall-mounted stands dotted throughout the hallways.

Rayna has ways of making people talk. She didn't scratch and claw her way here on looks alone. She's the best at what she does.

Any means necessary. That's how it goes. Showbiz.

Counting down to showtime, she inhales deeply, smiles through rouged lips, and fills her lungs with smoke.

"Good work, Anya." Still, she doesn't spare the girl a look.

She watches the final camera placed upon its mount and views the screens as one living, breathing organism. It has a pulse, eyes to look as far and wide as anyone could hope for. It has a beating heart, ears to collect secrets.

Elton Skelter

And the Phi Kappa Delta house has guts to spill.

CHAPTER VII

It starts making less sense the further through the terminal Elliot gets, one wheeled bag dragging in his wake as he wanders the endless bright-lit gates and neon-fronted shops. His hands shake, fear in part but mostly just from needing a drink. At the end of the trip there's a bar—or a bottle—or something, anything to make stepping foot back into that place seem like a good idea.

It's one night, one day.

And it's not the same place. Sure, its borders are the same borders that kept them warm and dry, but it also contained its own horrors, ones he was still recovering from. The husk of the Phi Kappa Delta house had rotted out after years of going vacant, the innards stripped away and repurposed for other places, the college itself barely survived that night. Inside, Elliot was sure that nothing remained of the place he left.

But there's a psychic imprint that lingers in a place, he believed that more than anything. He had felt the thrum of trauma when he'd gone back to collect his belongings, before he chucked it all in and returned home to Chicago to lick his wounds, physical and spiritual.

The closer he gets now, to Houston, to the Whitfield Campus, to the old Greek row, the more that same crackle of something evil, slick and greasy and insidious, paint the surfaces of his skin.

There's an announcement overhead to move to the gate and Elliot switches direction, moves against the crowd trying to exit the nearest gate. It sounds the chime to move on, forward to board, to mount the plane and fly the distance.

But boarding will take a while and there's a bar in the terminal. Time for one?

Elliot moves inside the bar-front and finds an open table.

One drink, or two if time permits, and that'll get him on the plane. From there, it's all down to the stewards and stewardesses to keep him calm and sedate, with the support of those little airplane bottles of liquor and the two loose Xanax rattling around in his jacket pocket.

He orders three fingers of top shelf whiskey, a Scottish blend brewed in a barrel for over thirty years and chokes it down without tasting it. There's twenty-five bucks spent poorly. He orders again, something cheaper and less exotic and doesn't taste the difference. He never notices the difference, save for the quality of the hangover he will get the next day.

From there his head is swimming enough to get through boarding without anxiety, his body floating through the motions as if he is not in control. He feels weightless as he puts his carry-on in the overhead, as he takes his seat in the window, as he absent-mindedly enjoys the business class offerings in his periphery.

He orders two drinks before takeoff, and as the plan lifts, Texas-bound, for a single lone trip, he feels free.

The feeling won't last long.

In just shy of three hours, the wheels touch down on the tarmac and the voice overhead announces their arrival into George Bush International. Something shifts in his guts. A part of him wants it to be a stabbing pain caused by his liquor-flooded insides, a scream of protest from a swollen liver, the first pangs of digestive distress.

But it's not, knows this feeling all too well.

People around him climb from their seats and pull luggage and accessories down from the overhead boxes, but Elliot doesn't move. He doesn't trust his feet to support him, wants to sit until the cold sweat across his brow subsides.

It's fear. Pure, adrenaline-shrouded, animalistic, do-or-die fear. It's inexorably tied to this state, to what happened a decade back, to what it was that made his life fly apart in the obscenest of ways.

He's less than an hour from the campus and the ice fingers of terror wrap around him, pulling him nearer.

"Sir?" a stewardess with a fake plastic smile asks. He grips his hands on the arm rests, blinks the sweat from his eyes and looks up. "Is everything okay?"

The answer, of course, is no. But Elliot doesn't answer her. He tries for a smile that barely appears, wipes wet hands onto his pants leg and climbs up onto his feet. His legs have cramped on the short flight, the tension sending waves of numbness and discomfort the second he extends to his full height. The stewardess watches with trepidation as he finds his rucksack in the overhead and pulls it down, inhales deeply and commences a slow march down the aisle.

Off the plane, into the airport. To baggage claim, to the liquor store out front where he buys too many bottles and asks for an opaque plastic sack to carry it in. As if he can hide it, the bottles prove him wrong, clunking heavy together as he walks out the front doors and into the dimmed sunlight.

And there he sees the car, a serious man in dark glasses holding a sign saying his name.

The tendrils of fear tighten as he climbs into the car and soon, too soon for him, he is on his way back.

Back to Whitfield.

Back to Phi Kappa Delta.

Back where it all started.

CHAPTER VIII

She doesn't want to do this. Priya has been trying so hard to escape the stigma. Bad enough being gay, but when your girlfriend wants you dead, it's a double blow. The plane rockets and rumbles beneath her and she finds herself praying for a fault in the line, nothing too serious, but enough to make an emergency landing. She imagines the lights and sirens of emergency vehicles fishing her from a minor wreckage, having to go back home and away from where she's headed. Hell, she imagines the spark of an explosion to blow her out of the sky.

She had dreams back then. Big dreams, a college career, post-grad, medical school, and all the way up. She fancied plastics or cardio-thoracic or general surgery, money and power and prestige. She imagined it was all enough to earn a pass for what happened from her family.

Instead, she's got PTSD from a killing spree that left

four friends and her brother casualties of a high school psychopath. And worse, she'd really loved her. She hated herself for the blindness, for not seeing it sooner.

It had been less than two years and she'd been fighting to survive. But without her family to support her, without being able to mix and mingle with new people and make new friends to replace the ones she lost back then, she was on her own. Priya had dreams, and all of them took a lot of cash to set in motion.

And then some woman calls her up, offers her some money and she can't say no. It's not nearly enough to get her through to the other side, but it's a start. Ten grand goes a long way to the next place. If nothing else, it'll offset the student loans, give her money to live for a little while before she has to double down and get a part-time job.

She'll be twenty-one next year. It's been long enough.

Rayna told her the money would be wired the second she'd done her part. An undisclosed number of nights in someone else's nightmare, sharing stories and wounds with a group of other survivors who lived through the same or worse.

And Priya feels guilty for thinking it, but maybe she can make a friend, someone with something to share that will make the last two years and the blood-soaked time before more bearable.

She tries to read a book and can't focus. She tries to listen to music from her cell, but nothing seems to match the mood. Everything is too loud and fast and happy, or too dire and depressing and lonely. Nothing fits, and Priya, she doesn't fit anywhere, either. Her clothes feel too loose and too tight at the same time. And Priya, herself, always felt like she stuck out in a crowd; one of the

Monomania

few brown kids, one of the only queer ones, the Hindu in a cabal of Christian kids. She was *other*.

She closes her eyes, flips to a breathing app, and works through her exercises. One long breath in for the count of ten, hold, and release slowly through her mouth. Over and over, breathing and breathing.

Soon the voice overhead breaks the Zen-like space she's shoved herself into and announces they will be arriving in Houston in t-minus-thirty-minutes-and-counting. It's not enough time.

The breathing hitches a bit, and she sees Claudia's face, first gentle, loving and kind. Then Priya sees the mask fall, obscuring her girlfriend's beautiful features, a hood rises to cover her molten red hair. She sees the gilt flash of a hunting knife poised to strike, and sees the blood spill, black in the darkness where her nightmares live.

It never leaves her. It likely never will.

And as much as she hopes and prays to whatever God she's meant to believe in, she knows she can never go back. Her brother's body cold in the ground, her twin, the other half of her, was taken in the violent furor. There's no going back from that.

The plane begins its descent into George Washington International and stays true on its course.

There is no turbulence, no sputter of an engine. Nothing blows and nothing smokes and the plane, despite her wishes, does not fall to the ground.

Instead, it lands, steady on solid ground.

And then it's too late to turn around.

Priya tries to practice her breathing on the move, but nothing stops the roiling storm inside. It's not her nightmare she walks towards, but it's still going to take

her back to her own.
>All roads will lead back to Claudia.
>Always.

Monomania

POLICE REPORT

Case No: 6546546546   **Date:** 07/16/2021

Reporting Officer: Det. Keri-Anne Webb   **Prepared By:** Louise South (admin)

Incident: This is the preliminary report of the spate of murders that occurred at Mount Rutledge High School, Pasadena, CA, wherein six students lost their lives. The sole survivor, Priya Ranganathan, who was connected to all the other vicitms, was found at the following address at the climax of the events and was taken in for questioning:

1254 Evergreen Lane, Pasadena, CA

Detail of Event:

Menacing phone calls to the witness commenced following the death of the first victim, 16-year-old Melissa Grayson and, when traced, the number was found to be linked to a burner cell, already discarded. The following night, Jaden Martin and his girlfriend Hannah Mortez were found slain at the High School. After the calling for a lockdown to prevent further crimes, a gathering of students met at the house of Claudia McGinnley, wherein a further two victims were slain, including the brother of Miss Ranganathan, ultimately revealing that Miss McGinnley herself was responsible for the killings. In a final altercation, Miss Ranganathan dispatched Miss McGinnley via bullet wound to the head. The origins of the firearm are as yet unknown.

Actions Taken:

Following a distress call from the residence, police were dispatched immediately, with emergency services called for back-up and to provide medical care. The call insinuated fatalities and the coroner was notified. On arrival, Ms Ranganathan was found alone, holding a firearm by her side which she was advised to drop, and which was taken into evidence.

Searching the property, masks, weapons and the afformentioned burner cell were located among the possessions of the now deceased Miss McGinnley.

Ranganathan was transported to the station for questioning.

Summary:

After interrogation and forensic input, it was concluded that the killings had been orchestrated by Miss Claudia McGinnley, working alone to terrorize members of the senior class of Mount Rutledge High. According to the living witness, who was engaged in a romantic relationship with the suspect, the reasoning behind the killings remains mysterious. Miss Ranganathan denies knowing any details of how the killings came to be and was released to the custody of her family. They did not wish to be questioned regarding the relationship between Ranganathan and McGinnley and asked for privacy while they contacted their lawyer.

Elton Skelter

Monomania

CHAPTER IX

The door catches as she turns the key. The lock disengages, but the thing sticks firm in the jamb. Rayna isn't shy about effort, but it seems a little off-kilter to have to barge her way into the building, particularly one she spent so much time and money restoring. The restoratives are all, admittedly, superficial, but it's the principal after all. If you look too closely, you can see through the new paint layers to the mold and mildew beneath it. You can sure as shit still smell it once the lingering stench of bleach starts to recede. Everything she's had done has been cosmetic, to the point that the original mattresses with their brown pungent blood puddles are still in situ. A bed protector here, a cheap statement rug there, and the worst of the costs were spared.

Rayna uses her shoulder and all the weight she can muster, and lays into the door, once, twice, before it gives and flies open. The smell hits her instantly, top notes of paint fumes and brush cleaner, but beneath it, the smell of rot. The smell of death.

Rayna smiles as she appraises the room, opting to breathe through her mouth instead of her nose. From the first time she'd seen the boarded up old frat house to now is like night and day. All superficial, but it will film great, and that's all she really needs. Never mind that she expects people to spend the next two nights here.

When she walks into the communal area, the old sofa replaced with something cheap but modern, the pool table restored and re-covered, she catches sight of the building manager, the small, unassuming man she knew she could trust to take all the necessary cost cuts on the work, and smiles.

"Bernardo," she calls to him, in a sing-song voice. She expects a smile in return but doesn't receive one. "It looks fantastic in here. You can barely tell where the bloodstains were." Only a hint of sarcasm comes through, half of her is being serious, almost complimentary.

"Sorry about the door," Bernardo mumbles, barely moving his thin lips curtained below a far-too-dense moustache. "I keep meaning to get to it-"

Rayna puts one hand up to stop him, and smiles. An idea starts to form as she watches the billow of her breath on the air. "It's fine," she says, and walks past him, through the lounge to where the restored kitchen gleams white beneath comically bright stage lights.

The kitchen itself had needed nothing more than a good scrub, simply by rote of the university's wise choice to keep the space easy to clean, to wipe off any errant stain or drying patch of vomit or food.

Or blood.

Compared to the carnage from the crime scene pho-

Monomania

tos she had seen the year before, when she'd started looking into its potential, the place is positively gleaming. Despite the deep, bone-chilling freeze permeating the room, it almost looked normal.

But this house? There's nothing normal about it.

She spins back to face Bernardo, takes a cigarette from her purse, and grips it between her lips, pulls a lighter and sparks the cherry. Bernardo looks at her wide-eyed.

"Uh, Ms. Rayna? You can't smoke in here?"

She blows a cloud of smoke directly towards him, watches him blink the plume from his eyes. "My man," she says. "I can do whatever the fuck I want." Her tone is as cold as the air around them. Then, suddenly, her frosty exterior melts and her smile returns. "Is there a problem with the heat?"

Bernardo follows her as she snakes her way past him, back into the lounge and back towards the door. "I have someone down in the basement trying to fix the boiler. It's been out of use a long time."

"Tell them not to bother," she says, and Bernardo cocks an eyebrow.

"But, the guests?" he asks.

The thought is taking form, has been a seed sprouting roots since the second she forced the door open. "They won't be needing heat. Just make sure they have enough blankets. And don't worry about the door."

This, Rayna knows, has always known, is not a retreat or a vacation. This, right here, is showbiz baby.

She thinks about the guests all set to arrive, the first already en route in the car she paid for, the man who outlived the walls of Phi Kappa Delta.

And behind him, all those broken, beaten victims

with their myriad disorders, all medicated up to the eyeballs, laser-shocked and therapized to within an inch of their pathetic lives.

The bleach-blonde tweaker who somehow survived the Cromwell Hotel. Those creepy twins the last to face down that Angel of Death Nursing Practitioner in New York. The camp counsellor and the heartbroken teen lesbian and all the other downtrodden little wrecks she'd be hosting.

Comfort is not what makes great television, but for these people, the lack thereof could turn the dial to eleven.

"Loosen some of the windows in the bedrooms, so they rattle a bit. I need more of the door sticking thing on other rooms. Let's get a smoke machine fitted somewhere out of site, and make sure the basement door is locked tight."

"Why Miss?" Bernardo asks, shivering in the coldness of both Rayna and the temperate house.

"Because Bernardo..." She lays her other hand on his arm, takes a drag of her cigarette, and lets the smoke out through her nose. "...I want this to be a *haunted* house."

Anya has stayed quiet for too long. She knows it, as she listens to the hurtful, unhinged way Rayna is basking in the glee of another's potential misery. This wasn't meant to be Five Night's at Freddie's. It was meant to be like Oprah, a show about healing, about facing down the darkness and coming out on top.

Anya watches as Rayna lists adjustments just small

enough to create an aura of fear around the already death-ridden frat house and decides she can no longer bite her tongue.

These people, these people *in particular*, had been through quite enough.

"Rayna?" she asks, and for the first time since she watched the woman shoulder-check the front door, Rayna turns and looks her in the eye. "A word?"

Rayna wears a sour look on her painted lips as she pulls the last of the cigarette and drops it to the hardwood, puts it out with the tip of her shoe. "What is it?" she asks, no attempt at pleasantry.

"What are you doing? I thought you wanted these people to tell their stories. Not *re-live* them!"

"Anya." Rayna's voice is stern and impatient, and Anya starts to feel her hands tremble.

"What could you possibly gain from adding to their torture?"

She's crossing a line and she knows it. But she stands her ground and watches red fury blaze over the older woman's painted skin. Rayna grabs her painfully by the wrist, pulls her towards the door and releases her. "You know what makes good television?"

Anya is about to answer when Rayna cuts her off. "I didn't think so. These people have all seen the horror of this world and lived through it. But it's about the horror. That's why they're here. You don't get to be the final girl and ignore the scary bits. We want them to come here and rip their fucking chests open, pour out their swollen, broken hearts for the world to see. We aren't in the business of fluff TV, and if that's why you're here..." Rayna, stronger than she looks by a mile, takes the door handle and yanks it open with one try. "...then here's the door."

Anya impresses even herself by standing her ground. She crosses her arms, mainly to save the woman seeing how badly the tremble in her hands has increased. "I'm staying," she barks, too loud, if only to stop her voice from quavering.

Rayna slams the door closed and smiles. "There's my girl. Now why don't you head up to the rooms and make sure everything is barely working."

She moves quickly to the stairs and doesn't look back, though she can feel the weight of Rayna's stare boring through the space between her shoulder blades. The space where a knife would fit if she let her guard down. With Rayna, it's always a possibility.

She stays, but not for Rayna. She stays because she knows fear.

And she stays with the hopes she can stave it off.

Just like before.

Just like when she was the last one standing.

When he sees her, Elliot knows it is Rayna without an introduction. She has the look of some aging gaudy news anchor turned behind-the-scenes shit shoveler. Everything about her, from the aerated quaff of her backcombed eighties hairdo, down to the rhinestones of her comfortable Payless kitten heels scream 'predatory.' Elliot has met enough Raynas in his life to know the look. She's got the razor-sharp teeth of a public prosecutor, coupled with the unscrupulous lack of empathy of a real estate agent. All this from less than ten seconds observing her.

She's standing on the sidewalk outside a cheap-looking faux-Chinese all-you-can-eat buffet place; a chain, not the marginally authentic types you can get down in a big-city China Town. The place is vaguely familiar, but no images break through the fog blocking his memories from that time.

When he climbs out of the car, the smell of deep-fried oil and MSG makes his stomach turn. He sways on his feet, the drive giving plenty of time for him to dip into the stash he procured at the airport, and even though he's glad to be standing, Elliot doesn't trust his drunken feet one bit.

"Elliot Hardy," Rayna says, saccharine and affected, arms wide as if she is going to envelope him in a hug that is neither welcome nor ever likely to transpire. Elliot grips his plastic bag in one hand, his carry-on in the other. "Leave the bags with your driver, he will keep them for you while we eat."

"Just you and me?" Elliot asks, trying to keep a cool tone to his voice. Truth is, Elliot would rather sit down to dinner with Ed Gein than this woman. He turns back to the car, to the open door he vacated, and slides his bags back into the back seat. The bottles audibly clink together as they touch the leather, and he can tell Rayna's expression even before he turns back to her.

"Everyone else is on their way," she says, reaching out an arm to usher him in ahead of her. "Let's get you *another* drink, shall we?"

Elliot blushes at the truth of the accusation and opens the door, the scent of processed slop a bat to his senses.

Remy jolts awake as the car comes to an abrupt stop outside some overly lit restaurant The mute driver glares at him through the rearview without a word, no sense of expression behind dark Ray Bans. Instead, he points one finger at the storefront, signifying that they have arrived. Rayna had mentioned a dinner but, for what he was getting paid, he figured something more upscale would be on the cards. But this was Rayna, and she was, if nothing else, a consummate conductor of delivering disappointment. If you'd ever watched one of her shows, you'd be hard pressed to disagree.

He climbs out of the car, abandoning his few belongings all crammed into an old JanSport left over from his niece's days at high school, and heads towards the door. Much like he had done for decades, he scans the area, surveils his surroundings, takes note of what he sees, a mental inventory that had done everything to keep him safe after what happened.

Back then, Remy would have walked into anything unprepared. He was just a kid, and life had yet to show him the darkness that waits around the next corner. He's not a kid anymore.

There's a car with blackout windows parked halfway off the curb to the left of the restaurant, its engine idling. Two people talk by the door, one is smoking what on first glance looks like a cigarette but smells like something stronger. Inside the restaurant, through the floor-to-ceiling windows, people have gathered, laughing, helping themselves to copious amounts of the buffet-style food centered at their tables.

All of this, and nothing too strange to carry on. The dark car gives him pause for just a second before a door opens and a young man climbs out on the street, looks both ways, sheepishly tucks his hands into his pockets and moves towards the restaurant. This kid could be a safe space to get him inside, he knows, and proceeds to move forward to match his arrival at the door with this kid. The two by the door turn as Remy and the young man draw up at the entrance.

"Excuse me, Ma'am," Remy says, addressing first the older woman, with a nod of his head. "Would you happen to be Rayna McCleod?" He nods to the younger of the two in the same fashion then meets the eye of the woman he spoke to. She inhales a full lung of smoke, exhales and clears her throat.

"No, I'm not Rayna, but I am waiting for her. We both are." She motions to her younger companion, glazing the sidewalk with the dust of spent ash. The smell of her hash is stronger the closer he is to her, and the scent dredges up a need in him. Weed was never his issue, but it's a spectrum, and he knows that, and after falling off the wagon and picking himself back up, the twenty-four-hour chip in his pocket is stronger than the need.

The woman sees him staring and holds out the joint, offering it to him.

"Oh. No thank you," he says, and reflexively, not to seem rude, she offers a hit the younger man at the rear, his hands still deep in black leather pockets, his bleached hair swept back, unwashed and unkempt. "I'm Remy," he says, to no one as the young man frees his hand to take the joint.

"Max," the boy says, pursing his lips around the joint, inhaling deeply and making no move to hand it back.

"I'm Lana," the older woman says. "Lana DeSteffano." She clarifies this as if they should know her name. Remy has never heard her name in his life. "And this is Dee," she says motioning towards the younger companion. It is only then that Remy notices the thick thread of red scar tissue running the width of this person's throat. He looks away before they notice his gaze. He has scars too.

"Is everyone here to meet this Rayna woman?" Max

asks, taking a second hit, handing back what little is left of the joint to Lana.

Dee nods their head but makes no motion to connect their gaze with anyone in particular. Instead, they look down at the tips of their sneakers, a wave of dyed black bangs forming a curtain across their face. They tuck their chin into the neck of their sweater as if they are cold, but to Remy, he knows it's to hide the scar.

Remy wonders if he holds the same aura as Dee, if when people see the scars forming tracks up the sides of his arms from the attack, they look at him the same way. Like a freak. Like a victim.

The door to the restaurant opens behind them, a rush of stale warm air billowing at their backs, and Rayna McCleod appears, backlit by the gentle glow of hanging lanterns and too-yellow downlighter bulbs.

"Welcome, everyone!" Rayna slurs, a few drinks deep, her voice too animated for true sobriety. Remy would know. "Come on in and meet the rest of the group!"

They follow her one by one, Lana at the rear taking a final toke of the last of the joint. She throws it to the ground, watches it swept away by a warm breeze, and lets the door close in her wake.

They walk, silently, to the back of the restaurant.

The night has begun.

Elton Skelter

CHAPTER XI

Elliot slams back another shot of Makers. At the request of Rayna, the server was good enough to leave the almost full bottle after the third refill, and Elliot's not worried about the cost, or how he might feel in the morning. He's just here trying to survive the night. He winces as the liquor goes down, hot and smooth against his throat as the room fills with what he suspects are the last of the guests to arrive.

Rayna leads them in like she's showing cattle at the state fair or selling trinkets on QVC, tottering on the heels of her tacky rhinestone shoes as she locates a seat for each of the new arrivals and snaps her fingers for a server to come over. You can immediately tell from the gathering who has worked in customer service before by the way they roll their eyes, or balk at the audacity of the woman.

This is the weirdest gathering of ragtag misfits Elliot's ever been part of. The age range for this group goes anywhere from eighteen to seventy-five if looks are anything to go by. Except Rayna. Late-fifties, maybe? A bad forty? Under the makeup and the dripping disdain for everyone she meets, it's impossible to tell.

One young server in a poorly fastened bowtie skitters around the vast table like a spider, scrawling drink order after drink order, pouring himself another shot into his glass and waiting to be led by Rayna. Since meeting the woman not two hours ago, he's got the impression that she knows exactly what she's doing. She's about as trustworthy as the food they are slated to eat. Hopefully, whatever slum hotel she's putting them up in has decent room facilities. He has the feeling he'll be needing them, one way or another. A bed's a bed, but a toilet, that's the jackpot when you find a good one. He laughs as he sips at the next shot. Like, who was he to know what good facilities look like? He can't even remember the last time he stayed anywhere other than his own house. He hadn't even once spent the night at Teddy's place, let alone in some random theoretical hotel.

This marks the first real time he's spent away from his house since dropping the down payment with the last of the settlement.

When the drinks have all been set down and allocated correctly, Rayna climbs to her feet and raises a glass as if to toast. "Thank you all for coming," she begins, and stops as if she has no idea how to continue. Elliot wouldn't have the faintest clue how to start this either, but he's not about to waste any empathy on Rayna. "Let's all introduce ourselves, shall we? I think once we know each other's stories, the night will be much...easier...to navigate..."

Rayna, of course, begins with the convoluted back-

Monomania

story of how she was once the face of the channel but chose to move into production once she'd seen all she wanted to see. The botched facelift that left her right eye slightly ajar, the way she aged out of demographic favor, the way she backstabbed every colleague she'd ever known; none of this comes up.

She finally sits, Elliot finishes the last of his drink, and the next in line takes their momentary place in the spotlight.

It's a round-robin of misery as the torch passes from one victim to the next, the sincere tears and platitudes of hope scattered among the weary tales of downward mobility, falls from grace, the lows and the lower stills. Rock bottom is a massacre survivor in a Chinese restaurant.

The food arrives before show and tell is finished, before the circle of death winds its way back to Elliot. Two spooky twins with matching hand-crocheted ponchos and equally artificial dentures regale the crowd with how they fought the big bad together, united. If it weren't so fucking depressing, it might even be inspiring.

But, the bottle of Makers Mark is two-thirds drained by this point and he hasn't the patience to dredge for humanity in the haze of a good buzz. He piles his plate with Lo Mein noodles and pushes past the urge to barf as a petite post-pubescent child tells the room how she survived the mass killing of all her friends when her down-low lesbian lover went berserk. That one's not a bad story, actually managing to pull Elliot's attention, and soon, the crowd is staring at him, eyes trained on him like the barrel of a sniper's gun.

It's his turn, and he doesn't know where to begin.

Where *did* it even begin anyway? You can't tell a story you can't remember, even though you were there in the thick of it. Even though you've got the scars as mementos. What do you say when you lose a whole night to trauma?

"I'm Elliot and, ten years ago, I survived a massacre in this very city." His cheeks swell in embarrassment. It sounds hokey, but that's what they want right? A good story. A tale for TV?

"So, you're the Frat guy? Damn, brutal coming back here, right?" Max asks, picking a hole in the sleeve of his frayed sweater.

"It's..." Elliot looks to Rayna who crosses her arms and lifts a brow. "...not ideal." He can't push the woman too far. There's too much money riding on it, enough to keep him comfortable until the next big idea. "I'm not looking forward to going back there. To the campus."

"Have you been back to Texas at all since then?" the older woman, Lana, asks, using chopsticks to prong a jumbo shrimp into her mouth. Her eyes are glazed red, and she seems more relaxed than she did when she first sat down, first opened up about '78 and the night she almost croaked it.

"Nope. And I plan to spend as little time here as possible. And even less in that house," Elliot says with a smile.

He's the consummate professional given his blood alcohol level, and he's playing his part as well as he can.

The tweaker rubs his hands through his greasy hair,

wipes them out on his frayed jeans. "Well, be hard to steer clear when you're sleeping there."-

His blood rushes with ice cold as the words land, slowly, in his consciousness. "What did you say?"

"What?" Max asks. "You didn't know?"

"Know what?"

Elliot can feel himself stand, feel the chair fall away behind him. "That wasn't...you didn't..." He turns his glare to Rayna. "What the fuck, Rayna? You never said anything about staying in that fuckin' hellhole!"

Rayna leans back, smiles wide, and looks up at him. There is a smear of pink lipstick across her teeth. "It was all in the contract, Mr. Hardy," she says, and the enjoyment she is experiencing from seeing Elliot falter is palpable around the whole table. Chopsticks are set down. Mouthfuls of food comically gulped. The room falls to silence.

"What the fuck is wrong with you?" Elliot scowls, trying to keep his cool but breaking out in a cold sweat, his hands wringing, his breath catching.

"Showbiz!" Rayna says and laughs as she waves her hands like a showman.

No one says a word. The silence is stifling. Elliot climbs over the felled chair and makes to leave, but Rayna, enjoying the power, the revelation, stops him dead. "You leave now, you're liable for expenses. Flights, drivers, loss of income for the studio. You leave now, and you get nothing, and owe me everything." She leans forward across the table and grabs Elliot's bottle of bourbon. "From what I can tell, you can't even afford the fifty bucks to pay for this." She uncorks the bottle and takes a swig.

Around her, people stare, some gloating with her,

others in horror at the sickening display of insensitivity. Elliot doesn't move, not back to the table, and not closer to the door.

"I...I can't..." he stutters, and she shushes him, lifts a hand to ensure the silence.

"You can and you will. Now take a seat."

And that's all there is to it. Elliot has met his match. Come the end of the night, he'll be back in that house, back where everything disappeared, fell apart, where his life ended with the end of everything.

He does the only thing he can. He picks up the chair and takes a seat.

"Eat, everyone!" Rayna rejoices. Slowly people unfurl from the scene, resume eating, hushed whispers between them as they ping pong their gazes between Rayna and Elliot.

Elliot reaches across the table and retrieves the bottle, sees the smear of her pink lipstick on the rim and doesn't care anymore. He takes a swig and meets her eye.

And the salt in the wound follows.

"Oh, and there's a nice surprise for you, Mr. Hardy. You'll be staying in your old room!"

Fuck, fuck, fuck, Elliot thinks, but he doesn't let her see the panic.

Eventually he looks away.

Some people are doomed to lose.

Isn't that how he got here in the first place?

CHAPTER XII

A mile down the street, past the cored out, hollow buildings, the college has a heart, a life, but Greek life has gone away. Even the sororities shut their doors when the massacre happened.

The main part of Greek row has been cut off from the rest of the campus. The buildings you can see from there are all boarded up. The university still technically runs, but everything surrounding the row is dead, like a bomb went off and everything in a certain radius was destroyed.

Elliot doesn't recognize the place, but the prevailing aura of death that hangs over it feels—somewhat—like justice. All that death and, like a cancer, it branched out, metastasized until it affected the whole damn system, and then brought it down.

End stage. No coming back.

Rayna's heels on the tarmac ring out in the relative silence as she leads everyone to the foot of the steps to the Phi Kappa Delta House. Elliot's breath catches as he looks up, the house larger than he remembers, looming over the gathering like some haunted monolith.

When Rayna reaches the foot of the steps, she pivots awkwardly to turn and face them. The elderly twins, taking up the rear, arrive just as she makes her announcement. "Welcome to the Phi Kappa Delta house. The site of one of the country's most infamous mass murders, and the place where our very own Elliot Hardy was spared from the onslaught."

"There aren't any cameras out here, Rayna," Elliot scowls. "You can quit the performance."

She lets the words roll off, pays them no mind, and starts to ascend the steps. They follow, lambs to slaughter.

When she reaches the door, Rayna must lean into it hard to get it to open. "Old wood," she says. "We tried to maintain as much of the original structure as we could. No worries. It's still functional."

Elliot watches as the crowd looks from one to another, not buying the spiel one bit. It's only been a matter of hours since everyone met Rayna for the first time, and it seems that most have got the read of her; untrustworthy, opportunistic, callous. That's Rayna, down to a tee. What was meant to be a healing pilgrimage with a cash reward is starting to appear more like punishment, like the money might just not be worth it.

Even Rayna's assistant, Anya, who has hung back and said absolutely nothing to anyone all night, is folded in a look of embarrassment, like the poisonous stink radiating off Rayna will somehow infect her, too. Honestly, her complicity is bad enough.

Anya had been the one who gave him the details and,

Monomania

now, standing outside this place he'd done everything in his power and a dozen things beyond to forget, he suspects she was just as careful to keep the final details from him, to bury them in small print in a contract he'd never have the patience to inspect.

He hangs back, waits until the last of guests has crossed the threshold, and takes a deep breath. From just beyond the doorway, he can already smell the scent of death, the kind of smell that would never leave your memory, if you had the memory to start with.

Lana notices the chill on the air as she rounds the corner into a typical communal living space, too-pristine couches without stains next to new rugs with their packing folds still heavily on display. The part of her that wants perfection, the part that locks the door an even number of times, the part that throws salt over her left shoulder when she spills, remains conspicuously silent during this. Her issue, it's becoming obvious, is liminal, caught only in the space where Halloween Night 1978 has embedded itself into her consciousness. Leave the area, find a new place, and the compulsions of that night take time to catch up. It's freeing, though she steps over the creases on the rug regardless to try and lay it flush against the hardwood.

Lana's breath is visible on the air and she pulls her cardigan tight around her and shivers. "So, the heating?" she asks.

"Comes and goes," Rayna replies, and that ends the line questioning.

The air smells of rot and damp. Deep within the woodwork, mold and fungus grows and spreads. The disuse of the building coupled with the sheer volume of products needed to clean away the blood has rendered the place a wet and sagging mess, spores infiltrating every surface so even the stench of paint can't reach it.

She looks around as the guests fan throughout the open space and notices the telltale signs of disgust spread as the smell permeates. Noses wrinkle and faces squint as the faint decaying odor reaches them on the chill air.

"You actually expect us to stay in this dump?" Max says, his words a slur. He makes his way to the now-closed door and turns the handle, attempts to yank it open but fails. "Fuckin' hell man. This place even safe?"

With a harrumph, Rayna clears the crowd and pushes him aside, grips the door handle and swings it open. "It's fine, it's all fine," she says.

No one's worry is assuaged.

For the first time since any of them arrived a switch flips in Anya. She steps up, blocking Rayna from view, and greets everyone, open-armed, radiating warmth. "Why don't we head up the stairs and drop off your bags so we can all get settled in?"

Heads nod, and Rayna, making herself known once more, scowls a response at the young assistant. "What a lovely idea, Anya. Thank you for your contribution." There is no warmth to the words. "And for your volunteering to do so. I'll be heading off, and if anyone needs anything, Anya would be delighted to help you out."

Again, Rayna scowls and turns and leaves, closing the door firmly behind her.

It is silent in the house, but Anya doesn't let it fester. Instead, she gathers those nearest and leads them towards the stairs. "Let's go, shall we?"

Behind the fake smile, Anya fucking hates Rayna McCleod.

For everything.

Elton Skelter

CHAPTER XIII

It's a hard ask to cross the threshold into that room. Elliot simply stands there, looks at the closed door and makes no move to open it. He hadn't even gone back in to pack his things when he'd left. That job had fell to his parents because he was in no fit mental state to step foot back onto the premises.

The bottles clink in a plastic bag at his side and he welcomes the calming sound of promised oblivion.

Eventually, he thinks. *There's no rush.*

Down the corridor, the other survivors have taken up residence in the rest of the rooms, the ones that once belonged to his brothers. The ones where their slashed and broken bodies were found butchered, and then wrapped in black plastic and carted to the local mortuary.

The ones where, he is sure, ghosts still linger.

The house thrums with the sounds of people opening drawers and wardrobe doors, the creak of old bed springs beneath the weight of new bodies. Standing there in the hallway, he hears it all, but he doesn't move.

Behind this door is everything he's been hiding from. The room where time stops. If he opens this door, will a floodgate of memory take him down? He wondered the same when he saw the frat house from the street, the same again when he walked in through the front door. So far, nothing had returned, but this was different. From every pieced together bit of information he had heard second hand; this room was where he fought for his life. This room was where the spatter of his blood lit the walls in furious red. Here was where the scars that now litter his arms and chest were born.

He could stall for longer, indefinitely even, but stalling won't change the past.

He reaches out, and as the clinking bottles hit the hollow wooden panels of the door, he twists the knob and prepares himself.

Nothing happens, but he has all night to let the ghosts come back for one last visit.

By the time she reaches the studio, escorted in the back of one of the blacked-out town cars that delivered everyone to the house, Rayna has sobered up completely. Despite warning her otherwise, she lights up a smoke in the back of the car, takes a deep breath and lets the noxious cloud billow into the upholstery. She doesn't feel bad, even when the drivers' eyes widen in the rearview, even when his face turns a caustic red in anger. She simply grabs her purse and climbs out of the back of

Monomania

the car, slamming it closed behind her without a word of thanks.

Everyone has gone home, and the offices are desolate, sterile spaces without the warmth of laughter or the comradery of her colleagues, and to be honest, she prefers it this way.

The ricocheted sound of her heels on the marble floors echoes as she traverses the slalom corridors to her office. When she reaches it, she doesn't turn the lights on, makes no move to make herself comfortable. Through the vast windows the light of the moon and the yellow glow of streetlamps give her all the light she needs.

She kicks off her shoes, finding comfort finally after a whole day wearing the damn things, and reaches onto her desk for the remote, clicks a button and steps back.

The entire wall of her office lights up with the glow of dozens of small screens, each showing the house in an eerie, blue rendering. She takes a seat on the couch, rests her shoulders against its soft cushions, and watches.

Since leaving the victims to their own devices, they have all found their way throughout the house. The corridor leading to a set of communal bathrooms is covered by three cameras all facing each way. The Cajun man, Deveraux, is making his way to use the facilities. In the kitchen, the creepy old women sit side by side drinking tea in unison, new matching shawls draped across their bony shoulders, their motions mirrored in perfect harmony.

Where the private rooms are scattered, along a broken corridor that curves through most of the upper floor, there are over a dozen cameras framing the location. Rayna watches with some glee as Elliot stands on the threshold of his old bedroom, the one from a decade before, the place she knows some trauma still lives.

Part of the reason she picked this place to pour her stipend into, to make it the base of this morbid union of terrorized former victims, was for this very reason.

Every story, of every one of these people, was documented fully, a narrative that started with a bad feeling and roller-coastered to disaster in the bloodiest of fashions. With every news clipping and recorded VHS report, every case had a start, a middle, and an end. You could novelize each of the occasions, write a treatment for TV with every one.

But not his story. Not Elliot's. Not in that house.

Something happened there and no one really knows the truth of it.

Rayna had fought to put the pieces together in a puzzle where half the pieces were missing. So many victims, and only one survivor left to tell the tale. A dead faculty member on site. A catatonic survivor with stress-related memory loss. What had happened?

Since that night, Elliot Hardy had never stepped foot back into Phi Kappa Delta. Not until now.

Maybe the trauma of going back would be enough to shake the memories loose. Maybe they will emerge over the hours he spends there.

Or maybe, just maybe, Rayna could give them a nudge.

She reaches forward to the coffee table, retrieves her purse, and finds the controller amongst all the papers and discarded wrappers. Leaning back, she stares at the buttons, refamiliarizing herself with the in-depth instructions Bernardo gave her.

Monomania

On the screen, Elliot puts his bags down onto the bed, the very same one he slept in that same night. Beneath the newly laundered sheets, beneath the mattress topper in thin memory foam and the cover to protect it from the user, there is a pool of dried blood caked into the box spring. None of that blood is his. Which makes no sense.

She watches him for any sign of recognition. In digital grain, Elliot runs his fingers over the surface of the old chest of drawers, inspects them for dust and wipes them on his pants. He turns in place and looks around the room.

Rayna watches all of this from the corridor camera, taking in everything she can.

Eventually, as she watches, Elliot closes the door.

She stares at the screen a little longer, waiting for him to re-emerge, waiting for any signs that he can't handle the pressure of being back in that room.

But the door doesn't open again.

She had stuck to her promise not to hide cameras in the room, but in this instance, she regrets the choice. Anya even talked her down from setting up microphones in the bathrooms.

She takes the control from her lap, finds the dial that corresponds with that room, and lowers the temperature in that room by just a few Fahrenheit.

When she's sure he's not about to bolt, she'll up the ante.

Until then, she wishes him a restless night's sleep.

Elton Skelter

Monomania

CHAPTER XIV

Lana pulls the duvet up under her armpits, crosses her legs between the covers and folds herself into as small a shape as possible to stave off the cold. The peppermint tea, the way steam rolls off it in waves, is doing nothing to fight the frost. She watched the young man hover outside of the room where he was attacked, and her heart ached for him. She had thought about knocking on the door, asking if he wanted to change rooms with her, but that was before she looked up, saw the density of cameras lining the upper part of the walls. She'd known they'd be there—they all knew—but seeing them was a different experience.

Everything, each minute detail within these walls, has been calculated and planned by Rayna and her team. One slight deviation and they get to pull the stipend. It was all in the contract.

Still, sipping her tea under the too-thin duvet, Lana wonders what must be going through Elliot's head. She doesn't know him, but she, too, has been where he is. If it had been the house where she was attacked, she doesn't know how she would cope. Everyone heard the glass clinking as he carried his bags to his room. Lana suspects, after seeing how he handled himself at the restaurant, that he had the ways and means to numb himself to the worst of it. She thinks of him in the frozen tundra of his former life, downing liquor the way she's slurping her tea.

If she weren't so cold, she would go down to the door and tackle it open, go out into the night air and smoke another joint. She had discovered weed was great for her nerves long after the attack, and though yes, it does help calm her nerves, what she likes most about it is the way it makes her feel like someone else. She feels like she could be anyone, anyone else, not just Lana DeSteffano, Survivor. She could be someone who doesn't need to do her routines, who doesn't worry the house will burn down if she doesn't remember to open and close the closet door three times each time she comes down the stairs. Being here, in the house of someone else's trauma, she doesn't have that inclination.

Lana climbs from beneath the covers, places her empty teacup on the old nightstand and walks to the window. Her hash tin clanks against the pipe in the pocket of her cardigan. If she can just open the window a crack, she can get this pipe smoked and air the room enough not to be detected. She can throw a towel across the gap beneath the door to stop it from going anywhere else. She places her hands under the little bronze handles and lifts upwards with all her might. The window doesn't move at all. Painted shut? She suspects so.

She leans in and inspects it closer, sees the place

Monomania

where the nails have been driven home. Have they been nailed shut?

It feels wrong, but in a house in as poor repair as this one, what could she really expect?

The night is dead-black beyond the window, and all she can see is her own reflection looking back at her.

A shutter slams somewhere down the house, in a room she can't quite place, and the sound makes her jump.

She takes the pipe from her pocket, balances the tin on the top of her knee as she sits and packs the bowl.

To hell with the smell.

There's something about this place that makes her feel…

Something.

Whatever it is, it's not good.

Meryl watches Wendy as she sleeps. The gentle rise and fall of her frail chest beneath the blankets soothes her. They are not young anymore and, to Meryl, every day extra with her sister is a gift. Especially after nearly losing her, after everything they went through in the care facility. Occasionally, between breaths, Meryl watches her sister still, then snort out a *honk* to release. It never fails to make her smile.

They had been sharing a bed ever since they returned to the apartment they shared in Manhattan, far enough away from that awful upstate complex where Annabeth Johnston had nearly taken Wendy out before Meryl had saved her. The altercation itself had been bloody, and

Meryl had had no idea just the depths of the situation involving the nurse and what the woman was doing. Meryl had simply wanted to save her sister's life when she'd seen the danger posed, had been arriving back from the bathroom at just the right time to see Wendy's bony fingers fight the pillow as it pressed down onto her face. Meryl hadn't been aware of how much damage you could inflict on a human body using only a stainless-steel fork, but the evidence had shown itself loud and clear when she had committed to enacting her rage out on the woman.

She hadn't intended to end a killing spree. But all that had happened afterwards—the reports and the interviews, the money itself—had all aided in getting them back home and back on their feet. Although now she couldn't sleep anywhere but in the bed beside Wendy.

It had been Wendy who, when noting how their money was running low, had suggested they take this last interview. Five-thousand dollars a piece was nothing to turn their noses up at and winter was coming, they would need the income to keep food on the table and the heat on high, less they freeze from the minus temps of snow season in New York.

And even Meryl had admitted, it would be nice to get away for a weekend to somewhere different. She couldn't remember the last time either had taken a vacation, and Texas had always radiated a nice charm to the twins.

When she finally closes her eyes, content that she has warmed up enough to sleep in this strange place, her sister's gentle intakes and exhalations white noise to sedate her, Meryl lets her body relax, sink into the hard mattress below.

Outside, frigid winds howl against the house and, somewhere along the huge range of the building, a loose gate or a shutter bangs rhythmically, something untethered in the unruly weather.

She closes her eyes tighter, as if doing so might shut out the noise as well as the remaining light from the moon beyond the window.

This house is old, older than their own back home, and with the rising storm outside, the way it leaches into the bones of the building and radiates inwards, the way it feels colder to be inside the house than outside of its protection. Every old bone in the frat house sings with each gust of wind and so the creaks seem normal and not out of place, even the creak of an opening door.

Meryl regulates her breathing, slows it down so she can match it with her sister. She trains her ear above the sheet, trying to drown out the foreign sounds around them so only Wendy's breath holds her attention.

The bed shifts a little, and Wendy's breathing stops.

Meryl waits for the *honk* to follow, but time draws on and the noise doesn't come. Neither does the shallow sound of her sister breathing in the bed beside her.

In the dark she opens her eyes, lets them adjust to the darkness, to see through all that black lit only by the hint of moonglow from the window.

Meryl blinks, once, twice, as the figure crouched over her sister comes into a dim view.

The room feels colder as she fights to find her voice, to find a scream, to reach down inside the well of rage inside herself and grab the feeling she had when she saw the nurse try to end her sisters life with the force of the pillow.

Her eyes dart between the figure and her sister and she pauses long enough to notice there is no rise and fall from Wendy's chest anymore. Her blood runs cold and, as she finds the scream bubbling up inside her, the figure releases Wendy's thin, birdlike neck from its gloved hands and pounces.

She tries to roll away, to put distance between her and the figure, but there is no moving, the longest train of her crocheted shawl caught beneath the dead weight of her sister's corpse. The scream arrives at her lips, but the taste of leather squashes it back, choking her. The figure is on her, straddling her, pressing down so hard on her mouth that it feels like her jaw might snap from the pressure. Her eyes fill with tears, one wrist is shackled in soft wool beside her, pressed beneath her and the rigid form of her twin.

The figure presses its other knee on her free arm and pushes down and she hears the crack of bone like dry twigs underfoot, thin and brittle. Then she feels the pain, hot and searing like fire. She screams internally but no sound comes out.

In the darkness, she looks up in time to see the figure's face, lit by a single sliver of moon, white latex cast against the red and blue of the stars and stripes. A mask, like a clown.

The stranger raises it's hand, like a Billy club, and just as her jaw gives way, snaps to the side beneath his grip, Meryl's eyes close against the pain, and the figure lets his hand fall over and over again. When Meryl stills, when the frail bones of her face fold inwards, when her eye pops from its socket and hangs against wilted, empty flesh, the figure keeps up its brutal pounding, their fist flying up and back, over and over against the col-

Monomania

lapsing crepe of the woman's battered skull.

There is surprisingly little blood from the attack, and the women, both so tiny and frail, will take little strength to move.

Behind the white mask with its patriotic decal, the figure catches their breath and slowly climbs from the bed.

By morning, there will be no trace of the women at all.

Elton Skelter

Chapter XV

Rayna had woken on the couch with a crick in her neck, her hair all flattened where she had laid her head against the brushed-cotton upholstery. Her lipstick painted half her face like a lopsided joker's grin and all she could taste in her mouth was stale smoke and cheap wine.

Still, she had woken early enough to get herself cleaned up before the big day. Once, Rayna had been the face of the channel, but this was an old boys' club, even now, and when her looks had faded, so had the amount of time she'd spent on screen. Production had saved her career, but she was still bitter about the hypocrisy, knowing the looks of the men who still got to remain on television, their sagging skin and neck wattles more pronounced than hers, unable to be covered with layers of screen makeup. How is it that these old men had outlasted her?

That is why this is all so important to Rayna. This deal, the viewership it will bring, the investors, the money. All of this will raise her profile in the eyes of the Network, and though she hates herself for jumping through these flaming hoops, she plans to reap the rewards when the show goes to air.

She is back in her own car, sober, recovered, showered, and fed, on her way to get the interviews underway. She won't be the one on screen, but she would never miss the chance to direct from the location, making history, bringing together generations of trauma under one roof to tell their torrid tales of survival against the most brutal killers America has ever seen.

If she was honest with herself, she hadn't thought the venture too lucrative when it came to conception. She'd been trying for years to get each of these poor little pin cushions on the screen, to pour their simple hearts out for the nation. The idea of bringing them all together and putting them in that grubby murder frat house had been a stroke of genius. But it hadn't been her idea at all. No, Anya had provided the thread that brought the whole plan together, though she had done as good a job as she could to gaslight the girl into thinking she had merely aided in the process. Anya, for all she was worth, wasn't that great an assistant, but the ideas that came to that girl's mind would be cash money if kept around long enough.

That wasn't the only reason to keep her around.

Anya had more than just ideas, but Rayna was keeping that in her back pocket to use at a later date, to draw on when she needed the ammunition.

Rayna arrives at the house a little after 8.45am to find the camera crew already unloading their gear, sees Anya at the head of the operation giving orders as if she were Rayna herself. It will give Rayna great pleasure to take

Monomania

over the process, if only to knock Anya back down a few rungs of the ladder she was desperately clawing her way up.

Rayna pulls her car into the lot beside a van housing one of the local anchors, a young and beautiful clone of what Rayna had once looked like, her pantsuit pressed to within an inch of its life, her face so solid with foundation that not a single crack could be seen. She hates the young ingénue already, but that's all par for the course when you're Rayna McCleod. Everyone is younger, everyone has stronger knees and a willingness to do all that it takes to get to the top.

Only Anya, it seems, plans on doing this the old-fashioned way.

Rayna climbs from the car, gives a half-assed smile to the anchor and makes her way over to where her assistant is directing the crew.

"Anya," she singsongs, the catch in her voice a combination of hangover and disuse. "How about you let me take it from here?"

Anya looks hurt for a second, but shrugs it off, hands off the file folder she is gripping to Rayna and turns to walk back up the stairs to the house.

"Anya?" Rayna says as she walks away.

"Yes?"

"Coffee, two sugars, dash of creamer. You're a doll."

Anya nods and stomps away and Rayna can't quite place what it is that makes doing that so much fun. Perhaps, she thinks, it makes a fine change to be the one in charge, the one with the power to punch downwards.

Whatever it is, it's narcotic.

With a wide smile through freshly painted lips, Rayna calls out to the nearest camera man, and insinuates herself back into the center of the commotion.

Back, she thinks, where she belongs.

Anya uses all her power to force the front door open and all but falls into the foyer when the wooden panel finally breaks from the jamb. She stops to stare at it closer, to see if there's anything that can be done to make it easier to enter and exit the property. To her surprise, the door frame has been increased by a fraction to cause it to stick further, wooden sheaths glued one on another to increase the width. Anya rolls her eyes when she realizes the lengths Rayna will truly go to creep out the show's guests.

She slams the door and turns to the interior of the building. It is much the same as the day before, and the guests, none of which are present, have left little by way of evidence of their presence. Anya takes a moment to center herself, catching her breath and letting the anger Rayna inspires within her dim to a small buzz at the back of her consciousness. Much like every other day, she will not let the woman get to her. It's a matter of principle, no matter how hard it is to maintain.

She takes a deep breath of the stale, moldy air and gags a little as Dee, the young, non-binary kid with the rope-like scar glaring from the base of one ear to the next, stumbles into view. Dee has their hands folded inside the sleeves of their chewed sweater, no doubt from the frigid chill in the old house, waves, feigns a smile as they draw to the bottom of the steps.

"Hi, uh Anya," Dee says, barely above a whisper. The

interview with Dee is going to be difficult to navigate if that is the loudest they can speak. Anya leans closer as Dee clears their throat to continue. "The twins, they left?"

Anya looks surprised by the statement but tries to keep the look from alarming Dee. "I'm not sure. Are they not in their room?"

"No," Dee replies, their voice cracking. "All their stuff is gone too."

"I'll speak to Rayna, see what's going on. I'm sure there's a reason." Anya doesn't believe her own words, but her train of thought is cut off as Elliot reaches the summit of the stairs and starts to descend, his feet crooked and unsteady. He looks, for lack of a better description, like he's still drunk from the night before. He holds one hand close to his chest, cradled in the other.

"What happened to you?" Anya asks, catching his attention. Her concern is less for injury and more for the liability lawsuit that will rain on them should the injury he's cradling be from some fault with the facilities.

"Eh?" Elliot asks, making his way to the foot of the staircase. "Oh, this." He holds out his fist too close to Anya's face, shows the bruising, busted skin around the knuckles of his right hand. "Got a bit…. overwhelmed. Staying in that room, you know?" Anya is glad to hear that the injury was self-inflicted, more so that he doesn't sound as drunk as he first appeared. The interview may not be a write-off after all.

Elliot, though he doesn't know it, is the draw for the whole show. His participation was the crux that pulled the whole thing together. Rayna had spent hours regaling Anya on the importance of this one guest. That's why it had been such a surprise to see the older woman so dead set on provoking him the night before.

Knowing Rayna, there was method to that madness. Perhaps she thought if she could keep him riled up, off kilter, that he'd be more likely to spill his secrets. Or, if it were true about his trauma-based amnesia, that setting him up on a rough edge might be the way to shake some secrets loose from that messed up head of his.

"There's a medic outside. I'll get them to take a look; make sure you haven't busted anything." Anya turns back to the door, then remembers Dee. "And I'll check about the twins too. Give me five. I'll be right back."

She wrestles the door open once more and does exactly what she says she will. But in the back of her mind, she can't help but feel something wrong. Maybe it's the house?

Despite all the tricks Rayna has laid, this place does not feel safe to her. Not at all.

CHAPTER XVI

Outside the range of the cell jammer stored in the basement, Rayna tries the call to Wendy's cell again with no luck. It rings a handful of times, then skips to voicemail.

"Wendy? Meryl? Where the fuck are you?" She doesn't try to moderate her tone. Even if she were to locate where the twins had run off to, she wouldn't have enough time to get them back, into makeup and in front of the camera before she loses the crew. "We had a deal, and we will be charging you for breaking it. Look forward to hearing from our lawyers. I hope you weren't planning on eating this Christmas."

It's cruel, but she doesn't care. At this point, the less she has to worry about, the better. The twins were just another slow-moving stress she didn't need. All that with the unpredictable Hardy and the rest of these misfit toys. Rayna's head throbs, no doubt the combination of low-grade booze and poor sleep catching up to her.

Still, the show must go on.

She watches as one of her medics patches up the damage to Elliot's hand and, in a strike of impatience, marches over to the man, intending to chastise him. When she reaches his side, she sees the strain in his eyes, the loss of his usual spark. She knows people. She knows not to push too hard. Reigning it back is hard work, but she does it despite herself. "Are you okay?" she asks, and he simply nods. "Wanna talk about it?"

Elliot shuffles in the chair as the young woman finishes wrapping the bandage around his hand, secures the end in place with a safety pin and departs. "Not really."

"Look, I know I was kind of a cunt last night," she begins, but Elliot cuts her off with a scoff. "But I honestly don't want you getting hurt over this. Tell me what you need."

He stops and thinks for a second, turns in his seat towards Rayna and looks up at her, her body backlit by the sun like some biblical whore.

"I could use a drink," Elliot says, but the wry smile on his face is enough to let Rayna know he's only half-serious.

"I think we've both had enough to last us a while. Let's just get through this day and then this time tomorrow, you'll be on your way back home."

"What?" Elliot asks, his face losing all warmth. "We are staying here another night?"

Rayna puts her hands on her hips, switches her position so he is looking directly at the sun. "We got in late last night. After the interviews, we need footage of everyone looking around, exploring the house, gathering in the common rooms. This show is about bringing you all together as much as it is about individual healing." She stops, then after a brief pause, places a hand on his shoulder. "And you could really use the healing. Has anything come back to you yet?"

Elliot shakes his head, and without meaning to, Rayna sighs. "Sorry I'm not having the flashbacks you dreamt of," Elliot scowls, shaking her hand from his shoulder.

"No, it's fine," she backtracks. "Maybe a bit more time walking around will help you get some perspective. Not many people get to face their demons like this. You should use the opportunity."

Elliot climbs to his feet and starts to walk away, back towards the stairs to the house. "Right now, I'm gonna use the opportunity to grab a shower."

Rayna bites her tongue and watches him leave, but such is who she is, she can't let him have the last word.

"Don't get that hand wet. And don't be late for your interview."

Elliot flips her the bird over his shoulder, and she drops the last of her professionalism. "And you better not have damaged anything with your tantrum. If I find any holes in the walls, I'm docking your stipend!"

He doesn't give her the satisfaction, simply walks up the stairs and into the house.

The crew set up various stations in which to conduct the interviews, one in the communal room, one in the dining area, at the kitchen island. Mobile stage lights have been set up to light the areas and for once, the house seems to rise to a reasonable temperature. The guests begin to emerge from their rooms one by one as if sensing a thaw in the atmosphere and before long, the kitchen is filled with them, all drinking coffee, eating pastries, and swatting away unwanted touch-ups from the make-up artists on site.

Dee leans their head back, tense as a ramrod, and allows the artist to start working on the scar. They had wanted to cover it over, maybe wrap a scarf around Dee's neck to protect the viewer from the ugly reality of their daily life, but Rayna had, as expected, interjected that the scar was the point, and that instead of covering it up, it should be displayed with pride. Perhaps, Rayna had said, it should be emphasized. Dee sits sweating their makeup off under the stage lights as the make-up wizards contour and recolor the thing Dee has worked hardest to disguise the most since the night of the attack.

By the time their neck scar is plumped and shaded and highlighted to a blazing perfection, they have to go back and retouch the face, mop the sweat from Dee's skin and almost reapply everything.

It'll take longer for Dee's interview to go to press. Because of the wound, because of the damage to the vocal cords that happened when their neck was sliced, their entire interview will need to be transcribed, subtitled, and it will take longer than anyone else's to find the right cut. That is the reason Dee is up first on the interview roster. They have yet to meet the interviewer, and the sound of their fellow survivors laughing and joking, gossiping like old friends around them is making them more nervous.

With the touched-up face all fine-tuned for camera, Rayna clears the rest of the group from the kitchen and

Monomania

stands behind the camera staring at the screen. She wails instructions like *filter with blue* and *get her a clip-on...THEM, get them a clip-on mic!* Dee simply sits there, trying to hide their discomfort, their embarrassment beneath the curtain of safety provided by their grown-out bangs.

Soon, the interviewer arrives, a tiny woman with fine features, subtle and intricate. Her face looks like some kind of bird, beautiful and exotic, but pointed in a way that doesn't quite seem natural. Her difference is what makes her so beautiful. Subconsciously, Dee flips their hair around their neck to cover the scar.

"Hair in the shot," Rayna screeches, and the interviewer and Dee both wince in unison.

The interview starts slow, questions about Dee, about how old they are, where they are from. Dee answers slowly, tries to enunciate as much as possible through the torn ruin of their vocal cords. They don't realize they are doing it, but every breathy and hyper-intoned word has them leaning down towards the clip-on, partially obscuring the scar across their neck.

"Cut!" Rayna yells. "Dee, sweetheart! We can't hear what you're saying anyway, so please just ignore the mic and keep your head up!"

Under the layers of thick, color-corrected make up, Dee's skin starts to flush, but whether it's from fury or shame, they can't quite decide.

The interview goes on, and Dee's neck starts to ache from the unnatural feeling of holding their head so high. Life with the scar had made them anything but proud, and the head-held-high attitude Rayna is searching for is not something that could ever come naturally.

From there, the interview presses deeper, into what

happened, into the night that Dee and two of their closest friends were attacked, how the attackers had targeted them for being different, made them afraid to ever speak of it again. Even in the recounting, Dee can't bring themself to say what occurred. That had been committed to paper once and any further recounting had become someone else's story to tell. But here, in front of this camera, with the birdlike interviewer, Dee feels the prompt they've never felt before, the need to recount the grossest details they had been hiding. Even from themself.

Dee feels their posture relax, as something inside them makes the decision that some horrors are not meant to be shared. Instead, they tell the story the way they have all along. Redacted. Watered-down. They allow themself to keep the worst of what happened because, though it was horrific, though it ruined their life, that trauma belongs to only Dee.

When Rayna finally yells cut, Dee can see, past the blinding overhead stage lights, that the woman is less than impressed.

Tough shit, Rayna, Dee thinks, as they strip the mic from their collar and move towards the stairs, determined to remove as much of the experience as they can from their body.

Rayna does not try to stop them, and Dee does not turn back.

Behind them, the camera crew move to a different lit location to hear a different story from a different survivor.

Dee wonders if that person will keep anything of their trauma back for themselves as well.

Monomania

MASSACHUSETTS INSTITUTE OF FINE ARTS

> This form is used to submit a witness statement regarding a pending case being considered by the Committee on Discipline (COD). Please complete as much of this form as possible. Detailed and chronological accounts are most helpful to the COD. Questions about this form should be directed to the COD directly.

Date of Incident: 12/24/2019   **Location of Incident:** Main Campus, Boston, MA

Name of Witness: Dee Vallanche   **Date of statement:** 12/27/2019

Statement: *As completely as possible, describe the events surrounding the incident, ideally in chronological order. Your description should focus on the facts of the case, including those that support the allegations of violations. You may attach and reference another page if you need additional space.*

Further to police report (Case*** 1274586) Dee Vallanche (they/them) provided this short statement whilst recovering at Mass. Gen. This record is transcribed from a written statement given by the victim to the police, due to the wound sustained to the vocal cords during the attack.

On entering the campus main at around 10.30pm on the night of Christmas Eve, 2019, inebriated and accompanied by four underclassmen, Vallanche was set upon by a duo of unidentified men. Two of the victims accompanying Vallanche fled at the time of the attack and were not present for the violence. The two who remained did not survive, one succumbing to injuries sustained from blunt force trauma, the other from exsanguination from a wound from a stabbing. Dee Vallanche has slashes across the neck, a deep wound severing their vocal cords and nicking the carotid artery. They were rushed to Mass. Gen when the attack was called in by a passerby, and Vallanche was administered immediate medical treatment for the wound.

This is being treated as a hate crime.

For further details of the timeline of the attack, as well as the identity of other individuals involved, access to the police report can be requested to permitted parties.

Supporting documents attached: **4 pages**

"Fundamental to the principle of Independent learning and professional growth is the requirement of honesty and integrity in conduct of one's academic and nonacademic life."

By signing below, I consent to my name being shared in this manner. By signing below and submitting this form, I also confirm that, to the best of my knowledge, this document adheres to those expectations of honesty and integrity fundamental to the Institute.

D. Vallanche

Signature of Witness	Email	ID Number
	d.vallanche@massfa.edu.com	54551684

Elton Skelter

Chapter XVII

"Hey, Tweaker, you're up," Rayna calls to Max across the kitchen. Max takes his time to refill his coffee, to push another croissant past his lips, dry flecks of pastry dotting the white Kleenex draped over his collar like a bib. Before he can finish chewing, Rayna is upon him like a storm cloud, slapping the croissant from his hand, taking his coffee and ripping the bib away, leading him by his cold, sweating hand to the place set up for him in the communal room.

"You've met, I assume?" Rayna asks, pushing him down into the hard interview chair and motioning at the interviewer sitting across from him, and slightly to the side. She doesn't wait for answers from either before she continues.

"This light is washing him out," Rayna calls back through the long room. "Someone take out some of the saturation or he'll look like a meth head." She has no tact, and for some reason he can't quite fathom, Max laughs. Like a tick, he fiddles the fraying sleeve of his sweater and tries to fix his eyes on the woman. Past the glare of the stage lights, all he can see is her silhouette, the back-combed hair, the shoulder pads, everything made gargantuan, made to look threatening. Max considers that if you took away all the embellishments, Rayna would barely stand a full five foot, that underneath all the additions of heels and layers, she is probably just a small woman, just like anyone else.

"Quiet on set," Rayna shouts, and the room falls silent. "And...action."

It's not a movie but it feels like one, feels so surreal to be there under the lights, that Max almost finds it easier to recount everything that happened in the Cromwell. The woman smiles with compassion and asks the questions with such a gentle voice, that Max could almost be convinced she cared for him.

"What was your involvement with the group, Max? Why don't you tell me what brought you there?"

It's not a hard question to answer, not really. The promise of somewhere warm to stay was always the crux of it. If they'd asked him what made him stay, that would be something entirely different.

He thinks longingly back to that last day, to Lillian, to the tears running down her face as her husband screamed at her, pulled the trigger. He cuts off the memory before the bullet hit home, something he can never forget but knows, if he gives into his demons, just a needle away, he doesn't have to remember, either.

The questions go on, never quite scratching the surface, all just innocuous enough to be intriguing but never giving the full account. That is, until the interviewer asks a question that can't be softened.

Monomania

"How did you get out of there alive?"

And there it was, the question everyone wanted to know. The one thing that was never widely reported. That it had been Max that had saved himself, when everyone around him had failed to say no, when everyone had gone with the plan and taken their own lives, Max had been the one to walk out of there alive.

But not in one piece.

"There were guns going all around us, everyone was taking their own lives, and Calloway had a gun pointed at me. After what he had done to Lil, he knew he couldn't trust me. I was unarmed, and I really had nothing left to lose."

"Are you saying that you killed Vince Calloway?"

A tear forms at the corner of Max's eye and threatens to fall. He nods, an answer, all the answer he can give, before the tear falls.

He looks away from the reporter, stares back beyond the lights and can see the overbuilt outline of Rayna rubbing her hands together. He'd given her everything she wanted. He'd earned his money. He just had to take it home.

"I was so scared, and I didn't want to die. I did what I had to do."

It didn't give all the details—not the way he'd thought he'd have to—before the interview fades out and ends. He didn't have to remember the second he took Calloway's head in his hands, gauged his thumbs into the old man's eyes. He didn't have to recount the way he'd pulled the man, blind, to the floor and smashed his head into the marble over and over until there was little left of the back of his skull.

He didn't have to remember that ever again if he

didn't want to, because now, he would have the money to forget. Back in LA he had a dealer just waiting to sell him all he'd need to forget for the longest time. Maybe this was worth it, after all.

Once the lights fade and the interviewer totters off to her next location, Rayna, with her overblown extensions puffing her up to look larger, comes over and lays a hand on his shoulder. "Not too bad there," she tells him.

"When do we get paid?" he replies.

"One more night in this house and I'll pay you everything I promised. You have my word."

Her word meant shit to him. But he could wait another day if it meant getting back to the way he was promised. He had enough gear on him to ride out the wait.

Monomania

Incident Report

REPORTED BY:	Ernesto McMannon	DATE OF REPORT:	03/25/2017
TITLE / ROLE:	Deputy Chief Officer	INCIDENT NO.:	5314684651

INCIDENT INFORMATION

INCIDENT TYPE:	Murder/suicide/cult activity	DATE OF INCIDENT:	03/21/2017
LOCATION:	The Cromwell Hotel, 460 Main Street,		
CITY:	Los Angeles	STATE: CA	ZIP CODE: 90014
SPECIFIC AREA OF LOCATION (if applicable):			

INCIDENT DESCRIPTION

Death cult activity reported by management of the Cromwell Hotel to the LAPD. When dispatched to investigate, the gathering barricaded themselves inside the hotel, armed with multiple firearms and began to commit ritualistic suicide. Documentation and video evidence found at the crime scene allowed for a picture to be painted of a hostile belief system shared among members who believed that their deaths would lead to ascension to another plane of existence.

NAME / ROLE / CONTACT OF PARTIES INVOLVED

1. Vincent Calloway (deceased)
2. Lillian Calloway (deceased)
3. 37 members of the organization (36 of which are deceased)

NAME / ROLE / CONTACT OF WITNESSES

1. Maxwell Von Dwyer – last surviving member of the Calloway Collective
2. Mary Rashid – Hotel Manager and receptionist
3. Carl Draven – Hotel guest

Max closes the bedroom door behind him and, much like the night before when he'd pulled down the mirror from the wall to cut lines on in private, wedges the desk chair beneath the doorknob. It's not a flawless system but it'll work well enough. He has hours until he has to leave the room and the sun going down outside the sash window will tell him all he needs to know about when to rise again.

It's just dinner and goodbye, one last sleep and then he's on his way.

Max sits on the bed and pulls his rucksack from the space beneath him. He rifles through the loose folds, among discarded tobacco packets and plastic bottles mutilated into bongs before he finds what he is looking for, a leather roll-up full of his gear.

Max unravels the roll-up on the sheets, the bent spoon, the box of needles, the tube to tie off the blood in his arm. There's maybe six hours until he has anywhere to be and the wound from what happened in the Cromwell feels too fresh, like a part of it opened when he started spilling his tale beneath the lights, like he sold a part of himself to the cameras. In a way, he guesses, he did.

He places the heroin on the spoon, just enough for the time he knows he has before he has to come around and be a part of this group again. He burns it gently with a lighter until the sticky black wad melts into a dirty yellowed liquid. That liquid, he sucks up in a hypodermic needle and holds it between his teeth.

Monomania

He sets the needle down beside the bed, pulls his sweater over his head, and settles back to tie the tourniquet around his left arm. And then he finds his vein.

It's not hard in the dappled pattern of track marks lining his inner arm. It's not as bad as he's seen on some people, certainly no worse than some of the others who had radiated towards the Calloway's and their cult in the Cromwell. Max knows he can stop at any time, but right now, he doesn't want to.

He plunges the needle home and lets the rest happen by muscle-memory and, finally—finally—that feeling in his gut starts to go away. Instead, starting at the crook of his left arm, pure warmth spreads out and over his body, his eyes roll, and he slumps down against the cushions, tries to focus on the window to watch for the movement of the sun.

All the pain washes away, replaced by euphoria. It feels like sex and love and excitement and joy, all magnified by a million, and every cell in his body sings with the sweet release of total oblivion.

The door to the walk-in opens just a crack.

It takes all Max's concentration to let his gaze follow where the motion appears, and it doesn't stop as he brings his eyes in line with the door. Slowly, almost painfully so, the door opens, a hand in a dark glove pushing it outwards, further, and further until it is flush against the wall behind it, and all that remains in the sparling aura of his gaze is a figure, a white mask like a clown over his head.

The high starts to sour as Max attempts to shuffle away from the approaching outline of this clown that steps further into the room. He opens dry lips as if to scream, but the figure takes an old shirt from the bed and balls it into his mouth, muffling the cries that, with time, might have erupted.

The bed shifts under the weight of the clown and Max is mesmerized by the stars and stripes pattern emblazoned across the forehead of the latex mask, the red nose, dainty but deformed, like a party clown but more threatening. The mask draws closer until it sits directly beside Max, picking up the spoon that has fallen into the folds of the leather roll-up. The clown liberates the last of the thick ball of heroin, too much to consume for one person in one day, and places it on the spoon, takes up the lighter and watches it melt until its black tar thickness bubbles into liquid.

Max has no choice but to stare at the display, like it's something unique or exotic, and he supposes, as much as he can in his current state, that the clown's presence is more than exotic. The word *menacing* crosses his mind, and the high dips lower and darker, feels like fingers grasping at his chest, constricting it, pulling him into himself.

The figure draws up the liquid in the same needle discarded from Max's first hit and fills it so that the plunger is almost hanging out completely.

Max stares in fear and wonder, frozen, knowing that if that much is put inside him, he will surely not survive.

The clown takes the hypodermic in its gloved hand, pulls back, and as Max follows its trail with his eye, it lands home. The sound of it piercing his eyeball is like stabbing a knife into raw chicken, and the bulbous formation slightly deflates with the contact. The clown pushes down the plunger, and the liquid floods through Max's busted eye, into the space beyond to mix with his blood. The needle perforates the sinuses, and a trickle appears seconds later, a globule dripping from one of his nostrils.

As it takes hold, Max can only see the golden corona of light splayed around the head of the clown, carved out by the sunshine at its back. But Max feels no fear. Not anymore.

Max feels joy. Pure, unadulterated, and brimming from every part of him.

So much joy, it consumes him, euphoria that pulls him away on its tides.

Max feels everything.

And then nothing at all.

When the life has drained from Max's body, the clown in the mask takes his body in their arms, lifts him up as if he weighs nothing, and carries him over to the open closet. They hoist the man's warm corpse onto their shoulders and shuts the door behind them.

Elton Skelter

Lana takes a moment aside from the frantic back-and-forth of the interview setup to apply a couple of eyedrops to each eye. She had taken a brief moment to herself during the previous interview to calm her nerves and the telltale signs of her marijuana usage had started to show in the red streaks of her eyes. She blinks, once, twice, and sighs in relief at the cooling effects of the drops, hopes it does enough of a job to calm her eyes, the way the smoke had calmed her nerves.

When she sits in the wooden chair, she feels her shoulders relax, despite the oppressive heat of the overhead lamps, despite the gaze of the camera people, and the turgid appraisal of Rayna. She feigns a smile as the interviewer sits down.

"I'm Annabel," the interviewer says, crossing her legs. "I'm going to keep it very guided, so just answer honestly and try to give as much detail as you can." Annabel places the earpiece under her coiffed hair and adjusts her jacket.

"Got it," Lana says, and tries for a smile.

The interview starts off slowly, a simple introduction, a brief recap of events, how long it's been. When Annabel says it has been forty-five years, Lana feels like she visibly ages on screen. Had her whole life seriously been wrapped up in this one event? Had she wasted all those years just to end up here, filming some hokey special about the people who live after their number was up?

"It was Halloween night," Lana says, shifting uncomfortably in the hard chair. Behind the glare of the lights, she can see Rayna placing her hands on her hips in disapproval and stills her squirming. "I was seventeen and I was babysitting for the kids of a neighbor. And that's when these calls started coming."

Lana recalls the venom in the voice, how it grew with every call, how it admonished her until she checked on her charges. She recalls seeing the nightly newsfeed on the TV, about people in the area whose houses had been broken into, how witnesses had seen no one, but a man in a white mask too tall to be trick or treating had been seen walking in someone's yard. She had turned off the feed to save herself the paranoia.

She tells Annabel that if she had kept watching the news that night, she'd have seen the other girls' deaths reported, some she knew from school, some close friends. She'd have seen the parents of murdered children cry for their losses and she'd have been warned. Instead, she had sat in silence and kept her eye on the stairs, listening for the slightest crack in the floorboards or click of a door.

When the last call had come, she had called the po-

Monomania

lice and they had done what they always did. They had told her she was probably being pranked, that it was Halloween and that people loved to play tricks. But the lieutenant she had spoken to had not seem convinced of his own words. There had been traces of worry in his voice as he'd taken down all the details and said that they would monitor the phone line and see if they could trace the caller. He had told her that it would take time and that she needed to keep the caller on the line for at least sixty seconds.

Another call didn't come for nearly an hour, and she had begun to relax when the phone rang. She kept her promise and kept the eerie voice communicating for over the minute mark, as told by her watch. When she hung up the phone, she had heard the first noise from the upstairs bedroom and gone to check on the children.

And to when the police traced the call to inside the house.

Lana recounts all of this to Annabel but, every time she reaches a pivotal point in the story, she finds herself being led further downstream, to where she faced off with the man in the white mask, to the injuries she sustained, to how she managed to protect the children and herself from the madman.

From how she eventually overpowered him, used his own knife to put him down. And how he had still gotten up and got away. The main points all seem lost in translation, and there is no telling it how it was. To Lana all her words sound empty and hollow, the story sounds so underwhelming compared to the monumental night she experienced which ruined her for her own future.

She hears herself say things like, *I lead a very quiet life now*, and, *I don't have many people who I see regularly*, and all of this comes down to what she has known all along. That she had wasted the last four-and-a-half decades being afraid to live her life.

This isn't catharsis, not like Rayna had said. This is mourning. This is seeing your life on a screen and it amounting to nothing more than…nothing.

When Annabel ends the interview, Lana can barely hold back her tears. She places a hand on the kitchen island and steadies herself.

"Are you okay?" Annabel asks, genuine care seeming so at odds with her previous aloof professionalism.

Lana looks at the knife block on the counter, the way it had been positioned in the corner of the screen the whole time. The way she was associated with the simple kitchen knife more than anything else.

She looks at the empty slot in the block and wonders if she'll ever stop having to take a knife to bed with her.

"I'm fine," she answers, but she is not.

Back in the relative quiet of her borrowed room, Lana reaches beneath the pillow to pull out the knife she had pilfered from the block on the kitchen counter. It feels solid and real in her hands, it has weight and gravitas.

But what it represents is far heavier, a prison she has let herself be locked in for all her adult life. The burden, like the knife, is a weight she never wished to hold.

She tucks it back beneath the pillow, grabs her purse and heads back to the stairs, the call of fresh air and other inhalants a siren song in her ear.

Monomania

Rayna, in her infinite cruelty, had left Elliot's interview until the afternoon, choosing to have him wait around uncomfortably, knowing he could not drain the remaining liquor stored in his room until after his appearance on the camera.

The most pressing issue of course was that Elliot, despite being in this house for as long as he had been, had failed to recall anything from the night of the massacre. When he walked through the doors, dread had welled inside him, and he had taken in the refurbished property with recognition and, somewhere deep inside, nostalgia. Life in Phi Kappa Delta hadn't all been about one murderous night. He'd enjoyed his time there, for the most part, even with the backhanded jokes at his expense, even with him being one of the only gay pledges who had made it through rush.

He stands awkwardly waiting in his room for the call, staring around at the chest which once held his clothes, the bed where he slept and read and fucked. Things look different now, of course, the walls all white where once they had been blue, the new rug covering the space between the bed and the door. Before, when he had lived in this room, Elliot had plastered the walls with photographs and posters, with tickets from concerts and cutouts from magazines. He'd pretended to love sports and had displayed a flag from the campus's many teams. This room, now, is just a shade of that memory.

Finally, as the afternoon winds on, the call comes and Elliot trudges to the door ready to pull it open. He stops, hand on the knob, looking down at the cheap Ikea rug. He wonders, why on earth someone would put a rug by the door.

Using the tip of his toe, he kicks the rug back and

the question answers itself. There, etched in the wooden panels beneath where the carpet had sat, the dark-brown amorphous stain has ruined the hardwood. For his logical mind to put the pieces together, it takes just a second, but when the dots connect, it hits him like a freight train.

Blood. So much blood.

For a fraction of a second, it's like he has cracked open a door, just an inch, inside his subconscious. He remembers a stain, though it is vibrant with red, shining with the sparkle of overhead light. It is not a decade old and sealed into buffed wood. It is fresh and he is standing in the center of it.

For a second, he remembers, and his stomach drops.

He shouldn't know but he does. The blood belonged to the professor.

And the reason it was on his bedroom floor, was because he had been the one to put it there.

Not all the edges align, and he doesn't let himself open the door any further. Instead, he slams it shut with force and closes off the past. Perhaps, he had been the keeper of what memories resurfaced all along? Or perhaps, it had taken coming back to start to put it all together.

Anya calls to him from the other side of his bedroom door and he jumps with a start.

"I'll be right there," he calls.

He doesn't have the time to examine what he knows. He doesn't even know what he knows for sure.

In an effort to keep himself together, Elliot pulls a fresh bottle of whiskey from the plastic bag and takes a large pull.

All he has to do, he knows, is say the same old thing;

Monomania

he just doesn't remember what happened.
    But in his mind, it's all starting to come undone.

Elton Skelter

Priya knocks gently at Dee's door, and despite the kindness of the woman's voice beyond the panel, Dee can't help but roll their eyes. It has been a lot, to go back to what happened, to tell it in an almost silent way that might not translate to someone who wasn't there.

Dee cracks open the door a few inches, just enough to poke their head through, and sees the small woman on the other side. Priya's face is red and puffy, tracks of tears have formed their way through the thick brown makeup the studio had applied to her face. Mascara has run tearful rings around her striking hazel eyes.

Dee tries for a smile, but they can feel how disingenuous it feels on their face. "Hi," they mouth with barely an audible whisper. "You okay?"

Priya nods but looks down as fresh tears pool at her eyes. "Long day," she says. "I just wanted to check on you. You disappeared to your room straight after the interview and I know it's not easy to talk about this…

stuff."

Dee is touched, but the thing they really need now is to be alone. Yes, the interview had taken its toll and yes, they were stuck in their feelings. But talking, especially with their injuries, had never been their preferred way of making it through the issues.

Without being able to acknowledge it with a full sentence, one that might convey to the woman what they felt, Dee simply places a hand on Priya's through the gap in the door, grips it with a squeeze. "Thank you for checking on me. Are you going to be okay?"

Priya looks lost, like she doesn't know what to do with herself now. She has rehashed something so painful for the world to see, something that will drive her family even further from her life, but Dee is not the person who can provide her the comfort she needs.

"I'm gonna try and get some sleep before we meet up for dinner," Dee mouths, and Priya takes a beat to process and then steps back, recognizing the brush-off for what it is.

"Sounds like a good idea. I might do the same. Come knock on my door when you're heading down?"

Dee smiles and nods and watches as Priya walks the length of the corridor, opens her own door, and disappears inside. Only then do they close the door.

Dee's trauma isn't quite as fresh as Priya's. But when they search their memories, they can't remember the emotions ever leading them to cry the way Priya had done since her interview. To Dee, the trauma wasn't a cause of hurt or pain, but more anger. Perhaps, since they had given so little depth in their interview, they had failed to drag up the past the way Priya had.

The truth is that they had clawed and fought to hang

Monomania

on to life, just to keep breathing. If they stop and admit that makes them anything but angry, then they know there will be further wounds to tend to. The scar running the length of their neck is enough to deal with.

Dee sits on the bed crisscross applesauce and places their headphones into their ears, searches for an overused playlist on their cell that doesn't require any internet connection, since there is none, and hits play.

Then they listen. The music is loud and throbbing, some EDM track they can't recall the name of, but one so frenetic and uplifting that they have no choice but to melt into the flow and relax. They inhale deeply and release the breath, timing it to the thrumming beat of the electronic drumkit.

Their eyes are still closed when the plastic bag cascades over their head, covering their face completely, adhering to their mouth and causing all breath to stop.

Their legs become caught in the sheets, held captive in a pretzel they can't shake free of. The body at their back holds them down, keeps them from moving, holds them there with nothing to do but fight in place. Their fingertips graze the outside of the plastic, but it does not give.

Dee can't tell if they are able to let out a scream beyond the pounding of the music in their ears, but solid, rough arms pull the plastic so tight, they can't get a grip to pull it away, to tear or free themself, to get oxygen. Their eyes start to bulge and redden beneath the opaque plastic, and they see nothing as they fight the assailant at their back, the one taking their life.

Dee had once fought valiantly and with extreme violence to make it through to the next day. Today, however, the fight just isn't there.

Their eyes start to falter, vision going black inside blackness.

No breath comes and, today, there is no tomorrow.

Anya can feel every ounce of venom in Rayna's words, flecks of spittle flying off with every vulgarity she utters. "Can you believe the vague bullshit he was spouting? I'm half inclined to not pay him for that!"

Anya takes a breath before she replies. "He did what he came here to do with what he has. You can't fault him that."

"I can do what I *fucking* like, Anya! And do you really believe that trauma amnesia bullshit? Come the fuck on. Something happened in this house and he's just not giving up the goods!"

Rayna's face is starting to flush the same hot pink of her manicure, and it takes everything she has for Anya not to shake the woman. It wouldn't be good for her job, she reminds herself.

"I'm going to have to edit the shit out of that to get to be half as interesting as it needs to be!" Rayna screeches a touch too loudly. From across the room, Anya meets Elliot's eye and makes an expression of sympathy, as if it will do any good. His face, too, takes on the shade of Rayna's claws.

"You've got all the pre-refurb footage you can cut it with, and there's the police reports. It's unsolved mysteries 101. We can get some pictures of the victims and make some wild speculation. It'll be fine."

"Do not handle me," Rayna scowls, but visibly relaxes. "I need to get out of here. I'm going back to the office to rewatch that mess and see what else we can possibly rinse from that cagey little queer."

Anya winces at the slur and places a calming hand on Rayna's arm. "Let me finish up here. If you need any more, just come back and I'm sure we can shoot it. We can have them do some diary room Big Brother shit, or something. It's going to be great. I promise."

Rayna looks Anya up and down with a sneer. "Fine, you finish up here, get everyone out and then I'll head off."

Anya nods and turns to face the mouth of the doorway. "That's a wrap everyone. Good job."

Rayna watches on with a half-baked smile pressed into her face as the camera crews pack up their rigs and the lighting is all taken down. With the absence of the overheads, the house is cast in an eerie pre-evening shade. Rayna shivers.

When the last of the crew have left, and Annabel has driven away, Rayna finally relents.

"That's it. I'm going to take off. Get them some takeout or something? You'll have to go into the parking lot to get signal."

"I've got it. Don't worry," Anya says in her most soothing voice, like she's handling a wild animal cornered.

Rayna simply sucks her teeth and turns, walking to the main door and all but ripping it off its hinges.

As the sun starts to dip outside the frat house, Rayna notes the silhouettes of Remy and Lana on the steps, their heads close together as if conspiring, fragrant plumes of hash billowing from around them. "Still not legal in this state," she admonishes as she steps over the half-empty cup of coffee next to Remy's leg.

"I won't tell if you won't," he says, but it does not draw a smile from the woman.

"Anya's going to order dinner. Why don't you go back inside and put in your requests?"

Neither Lana nor Remy take this as a request, standing up and turning back to the house. "And give me that," Rayna scowls as they disappear back inside. She takes the joint and pulls a long drag from the spit-slicked roach.

As the sun fades, the house starts to look less finished. There are cracks they never managed to cover, old boarded-up doors to subterranean levels they never had the time to explore.

This was all a mistake. The money won't be worth the output.

She takes another drag and inhales as inspiration hits her.

And for the sake of the show, for the sake of ratings, Rayna places the key in the only functioning door in the house.

And locks it tight.

As she walks away, she smiles. Show-biz baby. Here, we make our own entertainment.

CHAPTER XX

Priya had not managed to sleep in the intervening hours, nor had she managed to stop crying. There is an inbuilt misery to the frat house that has seeped into its bones and, everywhere she looks, she can feel something terrible. She realized this even before she located the space beneath the bed where a patch of thick brown had seeped into the floorboards, marking the room with an indelible stripe of aged gore.

Her tears then shifted from hopeless to horrified, and when she hears the call of Anya from the top of the stairs, beckoning everyone down to the living area, she is on her feet and out the door without pause. She cannot imagine another second spent on that bed, hovering inches over where some terrible murder had occurred.

Priya had heard about what had happened here and, though it seemed in poor taste to gather the survivors here to record this documentary, she had never even fathomed that remnants of the tragedy might still linger. She storms from the room letting the door slam in her wake, and before she reaches the end of the long corridor, she stops at Dee's door and knocks gently.

"Dee, you there?"

Silence.

She doesn't know Dee well enough to enter the room, but she does so anyway, turning the handle slowly and gently inching the door open.

The room is empty, the sheets in tangles, their belongings set about as if recently used. Nothing seems out of place save for a screwed up black bag on the floor.

Priya closes the door once more and heads down the stairs to meet with everyone else.

She finds the majority of the guests around the kitchen island, Lana, Remy, their eyes are bloodshot and red, both barking with laughter at some private joke. Anya stands impatiently, checking her watch as Priya enters the room.

"Did Dee come down with you?" Anya asks. "Or Max?"

Priya shakes her head. "I looked in on Dee, but they weren't in their room. Maybe in the bathroom?"

Anya tries to keep her cool, for fear she might seem more like Rayna than she could ever care to. "Okay, I'm going to order some food to be delivered. Any preferences?"

They begin a back and forth about the best cuisines, and Remy takes out his cell to look for the best local options for Postmates or Uber Eats. "Hey, there's no signal here. Like, zero bars," he says, and it surprises Anya that they are only just working this out.

Anya tries to keep it to herself about the signal blocker not five feet below them. "Yeah, it's a dead zone, I'll have to go outside to call. Is everyone okay with Thai?"

A resounding yes spreads across the room. "Shouldn't we wait for the others?" Priya asks.

"I'll order a bunch of stuff, there will be plenty to pick from," she says and leaves the room, that Rayna McCleod feeling starting to seep into every stride she takes.

When Anya reaches the door, she prepares herself to pull hard against the thickened jamb that keeps it from moving smoothly. She tries the amount of pressure she put in last time, but the door doesn't budge.

When she tries again, she puts all her energy behind pulling it open, but where the door had moved before, now it is fastened in place.

She bends down to look at the lock and sees the deadbolt splayed closed in the finite gap between door and wood.

Fucking Rayna, she thinks.

"What's wrong?" Priya asks from behind her.

There's no point in causing a commotion, so she looks back at the girl and smiles. There are still tracks in the girl's makeup where tears have run their way through it. "It's fine, I think we just got locked in."

From behind Priya, Remy and Lana stumble into the entryway.

"Did you say we're locked in?" Lana asks, suddenly sobered.

"I'm sure Rayna will be back any minute."

Even Anya doesn't believe the tone of her statement.

Rayna is barely halfway back to the studio when the

pangs of regret start to set in. Aside from anything else, what she'd just done was create a safety hazard. If a fire were to break out, the studio would be liable, and her neck would be on the line. She thinks about turning around, going back and hoping no one has noticed or that she can put the locked door down as a clumsy mistake; silly old Rayna got her thoughts mixed up again. But no, she keeps driving, the part of her capable of compassion silenced by the larger part who lives just to set the scene.

Traffic out of downtown is non-existent and she makes it back to the studio before she's even finished second-guessing her second-guess. She pulls into the lot, sees only a handful of cars dotted about the open space, and takes her usual spot right by the entrance. She's been using the same spot for years now, but it didn't come easy. She had to be trouble to get that spot. She had to have bigger balls than the old boys' club. She didn't find it hard to be the bitch. It came naturally.

The sun sits perched on the horizon as she lets herself back into the building and clomps down the slalom of corridors and back to her office.

There's no tape this time, nothing to scroll or reel through, nothing to cut and splice in the editing suite. Everything now is digital, direct access to everything that was filmed on site, now available at a different location.

The throb of the threatening headache from dealing with Elliot Hardy has started to wane the further she gets from the frat house, but the thought of scrolling through his ridiculous interview is bringing it back. Auras appear at the sides of her vision. A migraine is coming.

Monomania

She sets her purse and keys down on her desk when she reaches the office, flicks on a low table lamp instead of the mean halogen overheads. She does everything she can to keep the headache at bay. Then, she fishes out a couple aspirin from her desk drawer, pours herself a Scotch and washes it all down, pre-emptive action to an expected issue. That's what she does, puts out fires before they spread.

She looks up at the wall of screens at the far end of the room. She'd left them on the hours before, and they still blinked and fizzed with every static run of the surveillance ones, stark contrast to the crisp HD of the footage shot on the Steadicams. The larger screens are fronted with large moveable wheels to help her scour the footage easily, and she rings back the kitchen cam as far as it'll go and watches the looping video scroll in reverse to where Elliot lights the screen.

She casts a gaze over to the live cams, the ones dotting the hallways up by the rooms, the ones mounted at every high angle available in the concentric layout of the downstairs. A single screen goes blank.

Ignoring it, Rayna looks to the camera focused on the front door, aimed downwards and slightly to the left. She can't help but smile as she watches Anya turn the knob one way and another, watch her yank and pull with all her might until she all but wrenches her shoulder from the socket.

In another screen she watches the small woman, Priya, try to pry open the sash windows at the front of the house. The windows, after years of disuse, had been nailed shut and painted over, forced security in the absence of anything more hard wearing. The sight is comedic.

Another screen goes black, then another. It's subtle, but enough to pull Rayna's focus. She stares along the top row of screens. The three screens now black, without power, are all along the top corridor where the guest rooms lie. Another screen dies.

Then another.

Rayna takes the controller from the desk and starts to press buttons, unsure what anything does, but determined to bring life back to the monitors. Nothing happens as more blink out and fade to nothing.

"What the fuck?" she whispers, pulling her cell from her purse. She fingers through her contacts, finds Anya's name and tries the call. It doesn't connect.

She remembers the cell blocker and curses the idea. She was stupid to have put the contraption in the house. What if something were to happen? She curses, hangs up and places the cell in her pocket.

Three more screens along the top corridor blink out, replaced by static fuzz, then nothing.

In the downstairs monitors, the guests are still trying to jimmy open doors and windows, still looking frantic and trapped, like fireflies in a jar. She watches as Priya disappears and reappears carrying some kitchen utensil to try and carve open the window paint. Rayna knows this is futile.

In the second-to-last remaining screen along the upstairs corridor, Rayna spots a flash of black, a hand perhaps, sheathed in leather, before the picture diminishes to darkness.

One monitor upstairs remains live, and Rayna keeps her eyes on it. She watches as if she can work out the fault simply by observing.

As she stands there, her neck craned to look up at

the screen, a figure steps into view. She almost verbally staggers, takes a step back, and stares. The white clown mask, the American flag painted across the forehead, menacing and disturbing and something she can only recall seeing in passing.

The masked figure lifts a gloved hand, waves at the camera, and moves out of the frame.

The final screen dies.

Rayna feels her skin prickle with unease, a drop of sweat runs cold down the back of her neck beneath her hair, trails down the line of her spine to land in the crook of her back.

Still, she stands and stares at the monitor.

A joke, obviously. She reasons one of the guests has had enough of the lock-in, has decided to try and smoke her out with an eerie charade.

But what if something goes wrong?

Instant panic, regret, and a wave of nausea cross over her when she realizes that she has to go back, to unlock the door, to claim it was all a mistake and take her lumps. She grabs the keys and heads back to the parking lot, still that lingering image of the waving clown in her mind.

The mask she has seen before.

She just can't figure out where from.

Elton Skelter

CHAPTER XXI

The whisky proves an effective analgesic and Elliot has managed to stuff the recollection back behind the walls he has cultivated. He had thought he had wanted to know the truth, but the abstract images that came to him have scared him enough to retreat back into denial. Elliot would be okay if he never remembered. He feels like there is something so terrible, beyond the body on the floor, beyond the blood, that whatever he recalls could break him. He is already beyond repair and knowing will serve no purpose.

He takes another long pull from the bottle, winces with the burn, and looks at the glass container. He has already drained half of it and his vision has started to blur, his posture slump. He paces back and forth, drunkenly swaying from side to side.

Below him, he can hear a commotion, raised voices coalesce into a vibration beneath his feet. He wonders what Rayna has done now. Something despicable, no doubt, that has managed to enrage someone. Rayna McCleod has many talents, but firefighting was never one of them. She is the one with the gas cannister and the match.

Placing the bottle on the dresser, tentatively stepping over the rug covering the rusty stain in the wooden floor, Elliot walks to the door and opens it, trying to make sense of the voices coming from below. He can hear Lana above everyone else, calling for order, asking everyone to remain calm. It fits her, he thinks, to be the one in charge, not simply because she is the oldest, but something about her seems authoritative, which is not something he had expected from this group of misfits.

He walks to the top of the stairs and looks down at the four people below. Priya is grinding a baking slice into the crack of a closed window, and Remy and Anya are stood by the door, their voices raised over one another so nothing can be distinguished.

"What's wrong?" he asks from his vantage point. No one answers, or even acknowledges him. "Hey!" he yells, louder, and they turn to face him. "What's the problem?"

"Damn bitch has locked us in," Remy says with a scowl. "No way to get outside."

"Windows are all nailed shut," Priya says, digging away at the wooden pane. "Painted shut too."

Elliot can do nothing but roll his eyes. "Anyone got her number?"

"No signal," Lana responds, and takes the tin from her pocket, sits on the lowest step, and starts to roll herself a joint. "Place is a total dead zone."

He's had enough; enough of Rayna's bullshit, enough of sticking around in this haunted house. Elliot wants nothing more than just to leave, and after this stunt, Rayna will have no choice but to let them all go, or face having some kind of lawsuit filed in response to her literally imprisoning them.

He leaves the rest downstairs to panic and freak out. He has one objective and that's to pack up all of his shit and be ready to leave as soon as the door is unlocked. And if it's not unlocked soon, Elliot knows he'll be drunk enough to simply smash a window and climb out. Damn this fucking place, he owes it nothing more.

He takes another swig of whisky and grabs his bag. It feels lighter somehow, like there is far less inside it than there was before. When he opens it to look inside, things are missing, things he, himself, has not removed. His meds are gone, his tablet, some items of clothing. Elliot knows for a fact that he brought these things and knows he hasn't removed them from inside his bags.

Someone must have come into his room and taken them.

He thinks about these people, strangers he's stayed with, how he doesn't know any of them well enough to trust them. Without locks on the doors, anyone could have come into his room and rifled through his possessions.

He remembers the cameras, all positioned along the high ceilings outside the rooms and, for a second, is almost grateful for Rayna's intrusiveness. If he cannot find his belongings, at least he knows she will have video footage of someone entering the room.

He hears a crash from the adjoining room, something solid and dense and, immediately, he pictures the strung-out drug addict and knows who is responsible.

Without thought, he leaves the room and walks to

the next door, bangs roughly on the wood with the base of his fist. "Hey asshole," he yells. "You been in my stuff?"

There is no answer, and he bangs again, feeling the thin wood rattle and threaten to splinter under his pounding. When he hears no motion beyond, he simply opens the door and walks inside, pleasantries be damned. The room is empty, no sign of Max or his possessions. The bed has been hastily made but, aside from that, there is nothing to see.

Rocking on his feet, he enters the room, walks to the dresser, and pulls open the drawers one after the next. All are empty. For the sake of being thorough, he strides across the room, pulls open the closet door.

For a second his eyes don't register the mass of shapes and colors within. Bile backs up in his throat and he chokes down the burn, makes room to make a sound, to utter a word, though he can't quite find a word.

The blood is thick and black under the light, flesh beaten and rendered blue and unnatural in the artificial light. A staring eye looks out around a bent hypodermic needle. Max's blonde hair hangs awkward, defying the way his lifeless corpse is bent through the small opening of the overhead hatch.

At the foot of the closet, the elderly twins are withered, blue and beaten. The smell radiating off them is sour and makes his eyes water. One of the old women's head is completely caved in.

And the blood, so, so much blood.

Elliot steps back, putting distance between himself and the scene, hoping upon hope that his mind will break enough to forget what he has seen.

Again.

He prays for oblivion, but instead the memories start to unravel. The house, back then. Back when he was just a kid. The blood on his hands, the professor's lips at his neck, the anger and rage and the guilt. It all starts to emerge, flicking through his mind like the pages of a scrapbook.

He trips as he retreats, stumbling over something poking from beneath the bed.

A foot, sturdy work boot attached to a tight jean. Dee's leg. He doesn't look too closely to see the rest of their body and its state beneath the bed.

Finally—finally—a scream bubbles up from his throat, but what comes out is pained and wet. It keens through the room, ricocheting off the thin walls, building and trembling with every bit of guttural fear that has spawned inside of him.

Subconsciously, to a soundtrack of his own screams, he finds his back against the wall.

The bile cuts the noise and his mouth spews tainted whiskey vomit onto the floor. It tastes of fire and burns his throat raw. His eyes shed tears that block the terrible vision for a brief moment of respite.

Lana appears at the door and eyes him, asks him a question his mind can't process. He simply points towards the closet and wretches another painful stream of thick fluid onto the floor.

Her scream is long and high-pitched where his was guttural and confused. Her scream snaps him from the mindlessness of his state, slaps him across the face and back to reality.

"We have to get out of here," he says, but she can't hear him through her screams.

He has no choice but to take back control of his body.

He rights himself, wipes his mouth with the back of his hand and pulls Lana away from the closet, away from the bodies twisted and destroyed and packed in the small space, the other beneath the bed he's not even sure she's seen yet.

He pulls her back until they are at the door and then slams it closed, grips her by her arms, and shakes her.

"We have to get everyone, and we have to get the fuck out of here."

Lana nods, understanding, but doesn't speak.

Anything set to leave her lips will simply be lost in the shrill pitch of her scream.

Elliot doesn't know this woman, not really, but in that moment, they are the same.

He takes her hand and pulls her with him as he walks on shaking legs to the stairs.

Elliot guides Lana down the stairs, trying his best to keep it together, though the vision of the bodies is still fresh in his mind. The way the old woman's head had been caved in; the way her twin had been strangled until her eyes bulged out of the thin, hollow frame of her withered face.

He thinks about Max with the bent needle sticking out of his bleeding eye and Elliot's own eye starts to twitch.

Anya, Remy and Priya are still in their respective spots at the bottom of the stairs, but all have turned to look at Elliot and Lana as they slowly descend.

"What happened?" Priya asks, and it dawns on Elliot how young the girl is. She is barely an adult, not even able to drink alcohol legally and she is weathering the second storm in as many years. He wonders if she'll make it through this time, or if this is the moment that fate has caught up with her.

"They're dead. They're all dead," Lana says, her voice cracking, barely above a whisper.

"What are you talking about? Who all is dead?" Remy moves slowly away from the door, towards Lana, his hand out in front of him as if he wants to comfort her but doesn't know if he should.

"The twins, Max, Dee…" Elliot answers, the pale pallor of Lana's shocked face a sure indicator that she won't be able to stay on her feet for long. Shock is setting in and it's a downhill glide from here.

"So, the twins never left?" Anya asks. "And the others…they were, what? Killed?"

Lana nods slowly, but she doesn't meet Anya's eyes and doesn't blink should the tears that rest there start to fall.

"We've got to get the door open. Has anyone tried the back?" Elliot switches into survival mode. There is time to process everything later, everything he's seen, all that he remembered, but right now, there is someone coming for them.

"It's all bolted shut. Rusted padlock. Thick wood. No budging it." Anya steps forward and takes Lana from Elliot's grip, sets her down on the step to sit. "You okay there?"

"I'll never get used to that," Lana says, and no one needs clarification. They all know too well what she means. The sight of death never leaves you, never gets less shocking. It haunts you in the same way a nightmare does, sinking into your subconscious, setting up house, and refusing to budge.

"We're going to have to smash out the window," Elliot says. "We can't stay in here. We need to get to a phone and call the cops."

Monomania

Remy starts to move away from the door, like he's searching for something thick and sturdy, something that can knock out the panes of thick glass in the front window to allow them to escape. His eyes are searching the far wall of the communal area, when a sound draws his ear back to the door.

The sound of metal on metal, a key inserted into a lock.

The key twists, and the lock retracts.

The door doesn't open.

Remy moves towards it, pushes his face flush to the wood. "Rayna? Is that you?"

When no one answers, he grabs the handle, takes a breath, and pulls.

It takes a few tries, but finally the door swings open with a sigh.

Rayna's eyes are wide and bloodshot, her mouth hanging open, the smallest sliver of blood trickling down her chin.

The shock on her face is almost mesmerizing enough that it distracts from the slash in her neck. Blood starts to funnel down the front of her shirt, thick like a sheet. Her eyes lose their fear, her expression fades, and she falls forward, into the doorway, dead.

Priya screams first, Lana backs up the stairs, and Remy gently leans down to check the woman's pulse. It's futile but he's optimistic.

A shadow crosses him that he senses more than sees. Slowly he looks up, and stands, his muscles heavy with fear. The masked figure glowers in the doorway, one minute on the other side of the threshold, the next he is right there. He plunges the knife, over and over, and Remy doesn't have a chance to yell, to make a sound.

The look of shock on his face as he dies mirrors the one that Rayna was wearing in her final seconds.

He falls, and the blood starts to pool around him.

Elliot grabs Lana and pulls her back up the stairs. Anya sweeps Priya at her side, climbing upwards into the house on the heels of the others. Priya is unable to take her eyes off the mask, the pure white latex with the huge red grin, the stars and stripes like a mark of pride across the hooded forehead.

The figure doesn't move but follows them each with its eyes.

The clown closes the door, prepared for the final hunt, prepared to paint this old house red once more.

CHAPTER XXIII

Despite the fear seizing in her legs, the low-down hum in her gut of familiar dread, Lana keeps moving, putting the three younger people ahead of her, her back to the danger. It had been that way back then too, throwing herself as a shield before the children, making sure that if her time came to go, she'd go down fighting, that she'd always try to do the right thing. She's at the top of the stairs before she dares a look back.

The figure is gone. Experience tells her that it does not mean they are safe. Being in this house is the opposite. How long had this person been inside? The bodies piled up in the bedroom couldn't have been a quick undertaking. And the twins, they were gone when everyone woke up. Could this person have been inside the house with them all night? Watching and waiting for the perfect times to strike?

She looks back for a fraction longer, sees the collapsed bodies of Remy and Rayna, the blood spreading out around them like mirrored pools. Somehow, she had forgotten that blood could look so dark, so soft and slick. She had forgotten the way it looked in the years that she had been rebuilding.

It's almost beautiful, she thinks.

Her mind is racing when she turns back to the three younger people before her, all looking at her, all waiting for someone to take charge. "They're gone," she whispers.

"What the fuck are we supposed to do now? We're stuck in here with a madman and no cell service." Anya's voice trembles when she talks, the adrenaline surging inside her. She feels like she could run a mile. She also knows, should she be able to, she could get away, get outside and call the cops. Her cell is just a dead weight in her pocket inside the house. If she could get to the door, they could all live until tomorrow.

"What are you thinking?" Elliot asks her, seeing her fall silent.

"You're not going to like it," she replies.

For the first time, barely able to sputter the words out, Priya speaks. "Please don't say we split up."

They are silent for a second, before Anya takes Priya by the arms, gently turning her body to face her. "If we stay together, we make it easier to get us all. If we split up, one of us can get outside and call for help."

"It's okay, Priya," Lana says, comforting the girl. "We can hide, get somewhere safe and wait it out until the police arrive."

Priya isn't swayed by the argument. The fear coursing through her, making her feel like her blood might explode from her veins even without the slash of the figure's knife, has her trembling. The cold is simply adding to it. "Please," she begs, "We could all stay together. Safety in numbers, right?"

Lana casts a look at the bodies at the foot of the stairs. "Time to move," she says, and they move.

***

Priya watches through the slats of the closet, trying not to breathe too loudly or whimper. On the other side of the door, content she has left Priya in a safe space, Anya makes her way to find her own spot to hide, leaving Priya alone, crouched in the dark, with only the thins slats of the door between her and her would-be killer. She lets the tears fall as she thinks about what she saw, the huge carved grin in Rayna's neck, the vicious way the man in the mask had stabbed Remy over and over, the quick and brutal way he had repeatedly punctured the man's body so there was no way he could survive the attack.

Priya places her hand over her mouth to stifle her sob, and watches as Anya, slowly and silently, leaves the room.

Keeping their backs to the wall, an eye on their surroundings, Elliot and Lana walk the length of the corridor to Lana's room. Before, when it had been the frat house, Elliot remembered this had been Noah Waldock's room. He had been one of the boys killed in the massacre. Elliot had never read a thing about the killings, but he had known everyone who died that night, even if he was unable to do the heavy lifting of reading the speculation about the why and the how of it all. Noah had been a friend, in as much as anyone in the house had been a friend, and he, too, had been queer. One night when they were both tipsy, they had kissed each other, but it had never amounted to anything more.

Elliot shakes his head to rid the image of Noah as they round up to the bedroom door and Lana, as quietly as possible, turns the handle and swings it open gently.

The room is empty save for her sparse belongings, and she steps tentatively through the door, Elliot keeping his back to the room and his eyes on the hallway. Lana checks behind and beneath the bed and opens the closet, finds it empty and breathes a sign of relief. "It's clear," she says, and she feels like a cop on one of the shows she can't bring herself to watch on TV. She wonders if in another life she might have gone into something like law enforcement, if even without the events of Halloween night all those years ago, if she still would have felt the pull within herself to protect people who couldn't protect themselves. Her gut lurches when she thinks of Priya and Anya hiding, relying on her.

"Make this quick," Elliot says, and Lana sinks to the bed and pulls the pillows aside.

There is nothing there. "It's gone," she says, her voice carrying the weight of her defeat.

"He must have known you had it."

Lana feels a shiver down her spine. "Which means he's been watching us this whole time. How else would he know I took the knife?"

Elliot spares a second to look back at her. "What now?"

Lana doesn't want to say it, but there's only one thing left to do. They have to make a run for it.

The way she is crouching, Priya's legs start to ache, pins and needles prickling in her thighs. She wants to get up, to stretch in case she needs to burst from the closet and run, but the sound would be too much. Instead, she sits where she is as her muscles burn and prickle.

She has moderated her breathing to slow, short breaths, her mouth hanging open a bit to avoid making any more noise than she needs to. In the silence of the closet, she hears the gentlest scrape of wood.

She holds her breath, sits forward slightly to peer through the closet door's flattened slats. Nothing moves beyond the door. Slowly she sits back, still with her breath held in her lungs.

In this second, she thinks about her family, how they left things, how she might never get a chance to tell them what their disapproval did to her.

Another crack of wood from above. She releases her breath slowly and looks up.

In the blink of an eye, the looped rope drops down around her neck and, as she inhales to call for help, the rope tightens cutting it off before it can form.

The sinister gaze of the clown peers through the darkness, as the rope tightens to a crushing force around her neck. Her hands go to the rope, fighting at it, her nails ripping at the skin where the rope bites her flesh.

As her vision swims, she is hauled upwards, the rope scraping the entry of the attic hatch as the clown-masked figure disappears into darkness and drags her dying body with it.

"This was stupid. This was really fucking dumb," Lana repeats. Splitting up, hiding, becoming moving targets for this psycho had gleaned exactly zero in terms of levelling the playing field, and without the knife to defend themselves, all they had was each other.

"We should go and find them," Elliot says in response, as Lana draws up behind him in the doorway. "Get Priya first, then we can find Anya."

They creep along the corridor, past the communal bathroom and into the room that Priya had been hiding in. The door is open but inside there is nothing to mark her presence.

Lana walks slowly into the room, checking behind the door, under the bed, surprising herself how spry she can be at her age when the adrenaline is flooding her system. Her heart beats erratically as she reaches the closet. She peers through the slats but sees only darkness.

Elliot follows her into the room, back-up if needed, and Lana swings the door open.

The closet is empty and dark. Barren, without anything except a single sneaker. Lana bends down and picks it up. "Priya?" she whispers.

The boards above them creak, and in a single fluid motion that knocks her back in shock, Priya's body, hung from a noose, falls from above. She screams, backs away until she is pressed against Elliot, and turns from the corpse. The girl in death looks too innocent, too pure to really fathom in that moment. Lana can't stand to look.

The floor above them creaks again. "He's in the rafters," Elliot whispers. "That's how he's getting around."

He grabs Lana by the hand and leads her to the door. "Where's Anya?" she asks, but she can't control the sob that follows. She couldn't help the young girl, and she knows she won't be able to save the rest. She lets the tears fall in earnest because what else can she do?

"Anya?" Elliot whispers down the corridor and Anya appears from within the bathroom. The sudden presence of the woman makes him stumble, but as soon as she is by their side, they are moving, as one, away from the bedrooms, away from the bodies, and trying as they might to escape.

Above them, footsteps follow their path across the attic crawlspace and, somehow, the killer keeps track with their steps.

The footfalls veer away as they reach the head of the stairs, disappear from above. Lana pauses and looks behind her, while Elliot makes sure that Anya gets down the stairs.

Lana holds her breath, blocking out any sound other than the ones behind or above her. All she can hear is the pounding of her heart in her chest.

"Lana, come on!" Elliot admonishes, already halfway down the staircase.

She waits a beat longer and turns back to him. "Go, now," she says, and makes to move down behind him.

She only makes it down a single step before the clown appears behind her, quick as a flash from the closest bedroom. She barely has time to react, to turn and try and flee, before his arms are around her, pulling her back up the staircase. He plunges the knife into her side, and she manages a scream.

Elliot turns back and freezes for a second but finds himself moving back up the stairs against his will, running towards her as the killer jabs the knife into the older woman repeatedly. He is only a few steps away when the clown releases her body, sends it cascading into him, toppling them both down the staircase in a mess of loose limbs and bloody body parts. They hit the foot of the stairs hard, Elliot's ankle catching in the rails, bending horrifically away from its natural position. Lana comes to a stop on top of him, the fullness of her pinning him in place. Her eyes stare out, cold and dead.

"Elliot?" Anya yells from the door.

"Go!" he yells back. "Go, call the cops."

Anya pauses a beat and then turns, wrenches the door wide and runs.

With the position of his foot in the railings, it takes Elliot too long to free himself from beneath Lana's corpse. Her blood has drenched the front of his shirt, his hands are slick and sodden with her fluids.

He frees his foot and crawls towards the door, but the pain is too extreme, and he has to stop. Instead, he crawls backwards, back into the communal room, setting his back against the wall so he is out of view of the stairs.

He can't wait, but he needs a second to regroup, to get himself together and wrestle up the energy he needs to cover the small distance to the door before the figure returns.

He breathes, moves his foot a little and finds the pain receding into numbness. While he knows that's not good, that the shock is setting in, he's grateful for a break in the pain. He pushes himself up to his feet, the thin wooden wall behind him creaking with the pressure of his weight.

Elliot chances a look around the corner. There is no one on the stairs, no one within view except Lana's rapidly whitening corpse. Blood is still spilling from the gouges in her torso, but he can't spare the time to look.

Behind him, the wall creaks, louder than before.

Elliot stops, prepares to move.

The plaster cracks and the fine timber-clad wall crashes outwards, arms emerging from within the service space, a foot and a half of empty space where the clown erupts from, grabbing him and pulling him backwards.

The clown throws him to the rotting wooden beams below and he grabs for anything he can hold onto to stop the fall. His hands find the clowns' clothing and, together, they fall into the narrow gap between the walls and hit the ground.

The beams give way.

Underneath them is only dark, plunging them both down into the depths of the house, to the basement below, falling with the idle shards of destroyed flooring as the house around them screams.

Elton Skelter

CHAPTER XXIV

Elliot's ears are ringing as he lifts his head from the cold concrete of the basement floor. It takes a second for his eyes to focus and he lifts a hand to his forehead, wiping away the blood from the gash that is leaking down into his left eye.

As his vision shifts back to normal, he looks around at the dim light of the room. He tries to remember what happened, how he wound up down here. The sight of the clown mask offers a stark reminder. He gasps and shuffles back, away from where the figure in the ghoulish mask is out cold, a tangle of limbs on an empty surface, the remnants of the floor above and the timber frame through which they had crashed littered about him. Elliot crawls away until his back hits a beam, the pain in his ankle returning as it twists against his movements.

He is breathing too heavily, too loudly in the silence of the sublevel. Every breath rings out like a gunshot, ricocheting back to him in a deafening echo. He takes a final gasp and holds it in his chest.

The basement is sprawling, a wide expanse of unused space with nothing but old paint cans and garden tools propping up the unfinished walls. There is a single source of light, but from where he is sitting, there is no way to locate it.

He knows that Anya got out, that she had to have escaped. And he knows all he needs to do right now is stay alive.

Beyond where the clown lies, still and seemingly unconscious, there is a strip of daylight pouring through a vertical slit. A door, he realizes. Like those old storm doors that open out into the yard. If he can make it past the clown without making a noise, perhaps it can lead to his liberation.

He bites his cheek through the pain as he climbs to his feet, and makes a motion towards the light, towards where the clown rests against the cold floor. He walks, tentatively, not liking the way his footfalls sound in the darkness.

Only feet from his attacker's body, he spots the knife, covered in the slick blood of Lana, lying abandoned by the clown. Elliot inches forward, slow-step-by-painful-step until the knife is within reach of his hand. He steps a final foot down and...

Wood cracks beneath his feet, so loud he audibly jumps back. The clown lurches up and grabs his leg and, with the searing pain in his ankle, he yanks it free, kicks the man down until he is back on the floor.

This time, he doesn't stay there.

There is no getting past the clown, no making his way to the storm door.

Instead, Elliot backs away, watches as the clown picks up the discarded knife and eyes him in the dark. He straightens himself, cracks his neck, and motions forward.

Elliot turns and runs, forsaking the staircase that would lead him to the locked basement door. To survive, he needs to fight or flee, and he's out of places to run to.

He grabs a shovel, turns and, with a wide arc, swings it at the clown, striking him, just in the side of his arm. It's enough to fell him but not enough to stop him.

Beside the staircase, a wooden ladder stands against the wall, its top out of sight in the darkness, extended beyond where the basement roof stops.

Elliot doesn't think of the consequences, simply of getting away as the clown gets to his feet and retrieves the knife from the floor.

Elliot climbs the ladder, disappearing into darkness as the walls close in, thinning around him. At the top, there is a floor, and he pushes himself between the small space and lurches forward, crouched to avoid hitting his head.

Light shines through a single window before him, enough to illuminate the beams of the rooftop rafters.

The knife appears from the dark, stabbing into the wood by his foot as the clown appears at the top of the ladder and lunges.

Elliot backs away, not taking his eyes off the figure as it maneuvers itself over the last rung of the ladder and into the narrow passage leading to the attic. He is careful not to step away from support beams into the areas of thin paneling that make the bedroom ceilings below but, if he has to, he knows it's a quick way back down.

The clown advances, its blood-soaked knife like a beacon in the dark. Step-by-step, he inches closer. This is no longer a chase. Now, with the tiny purposeful movements of the attacker, the way he cocks his head, questioning what Elliot will do next, this is a taunt.

The attic stretches back for what seems like forever, and Elliot has to stay crouched so as not to knock his head against the slanted diagonal beams. He starts to lose the gap between them as his ankle aches and cries for rest.

The clown lurches, swinging the knife wide, and misses. Elliot jumps back, slipping from the supporting beam and stepping down onto the thin wood below. He moves his foot just as it cracks, and rights himself, using the rafters to balance.

In the distance, the ring of sirens creep over the sound of his pulse in his ears. The light through the window changes from the golden light of the dawning sun, to the red and blue of the police car cherries.

Again, the clown lunges, this time connecting, running a slash across the center of Elliot's chest, a red ribbon of blood bubbling through the torn fabric of his shirt.

Towards the sound of freedom, towards the police waiting outside, Elliot finds the nearest attic hatch and throws himself down it, into a bedroom below.

Where he expects to find hard floor, instead he finds the wilted bodies of the other victims all piled together. As he lands, the scent of death wafts up around him, threatening to choke him. He does not stop to grasp the horror. He stands on these bodies and moves, throwing back the door and flinging himself into the bedroom.

Limping on what now feels like a broken ankle,

Elliot stumbles from the room, hauls his ass down the stairs using the railings as leverage and down over the bodies scattered before the open door.

The blood from Rayna and Remy has thickened, started to seep down into the cracks in the floor so the wood is visible beneath it. He does not stop until he feels the air on his face.

He does not look back.

Elliot pulls the silver sheet around him, but still he shivers. They will take him to the hospital once all the wounds are covered, once they have searched the building for survivors that he knows they won't find.

He looks through the crowd as the EMT patches up the wound on his chest, sets a splint against his swollen ankle, but he can see no sign of Anya.

He hopes she got away. He hopes she is safe, maybe with the police telling them what happened, giving them all the details that will no doubt be mirrored by the things he will have to say.

He watches out the back of the ambulance as the police come out of the frat house, watches as a detective comes towards him, white as a sheet, a grave look on his face.

The man is silver-haired, thick around his middle but something about him is familiar.

"Mr. Hardy?" he asks. Elliot nods. "I don't know if you remember me. My name is Chief Laudermilk. I was the detective who took your statement…"

The recognition sets in. Elliot remembers the kind

detective for the way he questioned him all those years before, back in another life when he was a different person.

"I remember," Elliot says. His voice creaks with strain, his mouth as dry as dirt.

"Can you tell us who did this?" The detective seems less friendly now, more weathered, like the years have changed him.

"Did you not find him? The guy in the mask?" Elliot asks, panic-stricken in every intonation of his question.

"There was no one in there except the victims. We swept the whole building including the attic space and the basement. There's no one in there."

Elliot's blood runs cold.

He got away.

A second officer steps up and hands an evidence bag to Chief Laudermilk. "Sir, we found this in one of the upstairs rooms."

The Chief holds up the bag and examines the contents. Elliot balks at the sight. The clown mask sits inside, smears of blood over the white shine of the latex, mingling against the stark red of the stars, the thick blue of the stripes.

"That's what he was wearing," Elliot says and the Chief looks back skeptically.

The Chief turns away to address the EMTs. "Get him checked out. We will be by to question him once he's settled."

The EMT nods and closes the door, and Elliot rests his head back against the scratchy gurney pillows. He closes his eyes, knowing for a while, he's safe to let his guard down.

25th July, 2013

Elliot lies in bed, drifting in and out of consciousness, the attack still fresh in his mind. It's true, he'd been playing a dangerous game. Professor Radkin had been a running joke in the house, the kind of guy who would do anything for the forbidden. Elliot had used that to his advantage, but it was just a joke.

Or at least, it was until it wasn't.

The professor had become too aggressive, had pushed him until his back was against the door, had grabbed his wrists and started to kiss at his neck. He hadn't been able to escape, could still smell the lingering scent of cigarettes on the man's breath. It had all gone too far, and he knew it as soon as he had been called into his office, but even then, he'd never imagined the guy would force him to do something he didn't want to.

Radkin had taken one of Elliot's hands and pushed it into the older man's pants, had made him grip his arousal, had whispered in his ear what a whore he was, how he wanted it badly, how Elliot would get exactly what he wanted. Elliot had felt bile rise in his throat at the words, at the proximity to the man, and had had no choice but to apply a firm knee to the man's groin.

He'd gotten out of the office unscathed, but barely. He just needed to wash his hands, to grab a shower and to scrub this day off of him. He'd run all the way back to the frat house, locked himself in the bathroom, and scrubbed his skin until it was red raw. Then he'd taken the bottle of cheap booze on his dresser and taken a few rough shots. Soon enough, his head swam, his body relaxed, and he'd been able to close his eyes.

The door opens around 11pm. He only knows this is the time by the cast of the red light framed on the digital clock beside the bed. The silhouette in the doorway is backlit from the hallway and Elliot squints his eyes trying to identify who has barged into his room at night.

Beyond the doorway, nothing moves, no sounds can be heard save for the faint echo of the television playing too loudly in the lounge below.

The tip of a cigarette glows as the figure inhales deeply, lighting up the professors face in the dark. He doesn't speak, but he steps inside and stands over Elliot's bed, looking down, the smoke flowing around him like a veil in the dark.

Elliot sits up in bed, reaches over and switches on the lamp.

Only then does he notice the blood.

Thick, viscous red drips from the tips of the Professor's fingers, prints dot the white paper of the smoke in his hand. His eyes are red, shot through, and there is no humanity there.

"Whose blood is that?" Elliot whimpers, but his voice is barely recognizable. It's not the voice of the guy who baited the teacher, who played him like a fiddle and then walked away.

Monomania

The Professor smiles, chucks down the cigarette and stomps it into the floor with his foot.

The feeling, that electric feeling of danger, wells inside him. The look on the professor's face is barely human and he knows he needs to get away. Shocking even himself, Elliot lunges, pushes past the sturdy man and out into the hallway. "Help!" he yells. "Someone, help me!"

The door to the room next to his hangs open, the body of his frat brother, Devin Taylor, is butchered on the bed, his entrails slick, dead snakes falling from the cavity of his ruined torso.

He tries to rationalize the sight. It had to be a prank, right? It had to be a joke.

He stands still staring at the body a beat too long and, soon, rough fingers wrap into his hair, pull him backward and toss him into his room. The professor closes the door so he can't get out again. "What did you do?" Elliot asks, crawling backwards, trying to put space between them.

The professor follows his path, closing the distance, leaving Elliot nowhere to go. Without any chance to escape, merely wall at his back, he flips onto his front and army crawls under the bed, moving as quickly as he can towards the door. The bed above him shifts as the professor steps up, and as Elliot emerges from the far side of the bed, two thick legs pound down on either side of his head. He can do nothing but stifle a scream, to turn onto his back so he is looking up at his attacker.

The man's bloody hands fly down, grab the front of Elliot's shirt, and pull him up so high that his toes barely touch the floor. He had never known the man had such strength, but the way his balled-up fists hold him aloft leave no doubt that there is more to Radkin than meets the eye. He thinks of Devin's slain body in the next room and prays that if he meets the same fate, that it comes quickly, that he feels no pain.

He is thrown to the bed, landing hard on his back, the bounce in the spring barely cushioning his landing, and the breath leaves his body.

For a moment's grace, the professor turns away, walks toward the dresser, and runs his fingers over Elliot's belongings, tainting them with his touch, marking the boy's territory with the venom of his presence.

"I'm used to it, you know?" Radkin says, but his voice doesn't sound the same as it has, the way it did at the front of a lecture hall. Not even the way it sounded in Elliot's ear with his back against the office door. There is evil in his tone, a stoney, emotionless drawl that sends shivers through Elliot's body. "I'm used to people laughing at me. I've been doing this long enough."

"I'm sorry," Elliot whispers, and Radkin pounds his hand onto the dresser, scattering coins and empty beer cans to the floor.

"I put up with a lot but today just..." Radkin turns back, holding a mask, a twisted smiling clown in white latex, the blood-red grin and button nose, the forehead emblazoned with the stars and stripes. "There comes a point when enough is enough. And then the dean comes to my office..."

"I didn't say anything, I swear!" Elliot hates how vulnerable he sounds, speaking through tears, trembling with terror, the fullness of his bladder threatening to void.

The professor places the mask over his face. "I know, but he told me I was too close to the students. He didn't say it directly, but I know what he meant!" His voice is muffled in the latex, dulling his emotionless tone even more. He steps towards the bed, and one blood-coated hand goes to his belt. For the first time, Elliot sees the knife.

"I'll get the last laugh," Radkin slurs behind the face cov-

ering, and pulls the knife from his waist. With a lunge, he is on top of Elliot, straddling his hips, hovering above with the knife poised to strike.

And the man in the mask, baring down, the tip of his red-soaked knife set to fall, sets off a fire in Elliot. He throws up his hands and catches Radkin's wrists as he plunges his weapon and, using the surprise of the moment, bucks sideways, sending the man spiraling off the bed. Then, he's on autopilot, climbing to his feet, blindly reaching out to grab the nearest thing he can, his fingers finding the marble base of a trophy.

Then it is Elliot on top of the fray, Elliot is baring down, Elliot is the threat.

He raises the trophy high above his head and swings down, the corner of the marble base pounding through the latex, creating a rift for red to flow through. The knife is cast aside as Radkin's fists ball at the pain, the mask choking back a cry of surprise.

But—to Elliot—it's no longer Radkin. To him, it is a threat, some abstract embodiment of the things in the world that are out to harm him. He lifts the trophy and swings again.

And again.

And again.

The mask folds in on itself, the white becoming furious crimson, the stars migrating over the stripes.

He pounds down until the bone beneath the rubber breaks and shatters, until the spasm of the body stops. Even then, he continues to pound down and doesn't stop until the trophy breaks.

The horror does not stop him. Nothing does. His consciousness has set it aside for good.

This isn't Elliot anymore.

This is something else.

Elton Skelter

CHAPTER XXVI

It had taken days for the cops to allow him to leave the state, but Elliot finally arrives home, his ankle set in a fracture brace that itches every time he walks. The hospital had not been generous with his treatment, and the police had been relentless with their questioning, and it had struck him as strange that they knew nothing of what had transpired. He had expected, with Anya's statement, that they might expect what was being said to them. The face of the officers had stared back blankly as if he was talking a foreign language.

He is home, bags cast onto the kitchen island, when Teddy lets himself in the door, the scant pile of forgotten mail from the box cast underneath his arm. "You're home!" he declares, and pulls Elliot into an embrace. "When did you get back?" Teddy steps back, holding onto Elliot's arms and looks him up and down, letting his gaze drift to the wounded foot in the Velcro boot. He chucks the mail down onto the counter and holds onto Elliot's chin, turning his face left and right, checking him for the wounds sustained in the attack.

"Just got in," Elliot replies, laying his hands against Teddy's chest, feeling the solid strength of him, taking that strength into himself. "I missed you," he whispers. Teddy flushes, unused to the sentimentality, unsure of how to respond.

"You've really been through it," Teddy says. "Can I get you something? A drink? Something to eat?"

Surprising even himself, Elliot does not feel the need to drink. The memories shook loose from inside of him seem to have liberated some part of him that felt the need to self-medicate, and though he can still feel the horror of what happened to him, the last days and what he has been through has given it perspective. The monster that came out then had saved his life. The darkest part of him had given rise to his survival.

"I'm good," Elliot replies, and lays his head against Teddy's shoulder. "Now I'm home." He inhales, filling his lungs with the familiar scent of Teddy, of the man he loves, the man he might have lost had the tables turned differently.

"So, you remember what happened now?" Teddy asks, pulling him upright, a look of deep concern and compassion etched in the lines of his expression.

"I remember everything," Elliot says. He doesn't wish to expound on this but the look on Teddy's face shows him he needs to divulge more. "It was impossible not to. Being back there, in that house, in that room. It just all slid back in pieces. And then that mask..." He shakes his head as if the motion will expel the image, but it doesn't. It lingers there, tied with the regained memory, a clown on a rampage, men in masks who were hell-bent on his demise.

"What do you remember?" Teddy asks, tentatively, showing his support by the slow rubbing motion on the tops of Elliot's arms. "Tell me everything."

"I will," Elliot assures him. "Just, not now. There was a bad guy, he hurt a lot of people, and I did some things I'm not proud of to stop him. That's all I can really say right now."

"I understand," Teddy responds. "Poor guy."

Elliot turns out of the gaze of his partner, and moves into the kitchen proper, bypassing the island until he is at the refrigerator. He opens it, looks inside, and closes it straight away. He is not hungry or thirsty and he knows there is nothing inside. He just needs to feel at home again.

But there is something wrong, and he knows it. A masked man, wearing the same mask as the man he killed all those years ago, had come to try and take him out again.

Teddy watches as he starts to busy himself, resting his hips against the counter and picking up the mail. The last time he had done this, the invitation had arrived that lured him back there.

Lure. It hits a nerve. Was that all there was to it?

Something doesn't make sense.

Elliot rifles through the letters one by one. Bill, bill, bill, and, without the money Rayna had promised, no way of paying them.

One envelope is blank, a thick paper envelope with the flap unsealed. There is no address on it. He opens it and starts to read.

His face screws up, confusion, meeting horror, meeting recognition.

Teddy walks around the island to stand beside him.

"What is this?" Elliot asks to no one in particular, but to the one person who'll hear him.

"What does it look like?" Teddy asks, pulling the gun from the back of his belt and aiming the revolver square at Elliot's temple. "It's a suicide note."

Elliot doesn't get a chance to respond before Teddy pulls the trigger, and Elliot's brains paint the kitchen cabinets in an artistic spray of gore and horror.

He stands above the fallen body and admires his work. He had wanted to do that for a *really* long time.

Teddy wipes the gun on a cloth, places it in Elliot's dead hand, and sets to stage the last of the scene. The gunfire will no doubt draw the police in time.

He starts to unpack the stolen belongings, the things that will trace it all back to Elliot, things that belonged to the people who died along the way to the payback that Elliot deserved.

It's the last step, ten years in the making and, when he is done, Teddy leaves the house for the last time.

He won't be looking back, but he feels a hell of a lot better now.

I'm sorry,
I never meant this to happen again. Being in that house,
back where it happened the first time, it all came flooding
back. I didn't remember before, but I do now.
I was responsible. I killed them all.
I did it then.
I did it now.
I can't live with the guilt.
Please forgive me.
-Elliot Hardy

CHAPTER XXVII

He watches at the window, watches Anya skip the footage, wind it back and forth, erase, repeat. The sun is going down and the office that was once Rayna's is darkening under the growing shade. Headphones cover her ears, effectively deafening her to his approach. He smiles and opens the door slowly, steps inside, closing the door behind him. He knows she will scream; the door will muffle it. He'll be quick and it will be enough.

She is blind to the approach, cutting the footage into shreds, removing herself frame by frame, erasing her presence. From the darkness, he approaches, and with a sudden motion, grabs Anya from behind.

She screams.

Teddy's laughter settles her frayed nerves, and she slaps him on the arm. "*Goddammit*, Teddy! You scared me!" she says flirtatiously, but looking at his impish smile, she can't stay mad at him. He leans in and kisses her and, subconsciously, her foot raises behind her. His touch always has this effect on her, has done since the moment they first met.

"Is it done?" she asks, pulling back from the kiss, staring up into his loving gaze.

"You betcha, baby," Teddy replies, and is rewarded by the smile she radiates.

"I've nearly finished doctoring the footage. I'll be able to cut it together to fit the narrative soon enough. And then it's done. Then we're free."

He pulls her close and kisses her ferociously. It's all he has wanted since the plan first set in motion. It's all he could have asked for, and Elliot Hardy got exactly what was coming to him.

"He'd be proud of you, you know?" she tells him between breathtaking clashes of their lips. "Your father. You cleared his name."

"And took that bitch out in the process," he replies.

Rayna McCleod had been the draw for Anya, the promise of her demise had been spurring her on ever since the report aired that upended her entire life. It wasn't bad enough that she had lost her father, but Rayna's careless coverage of his death had driven her mother to the edge, had resulted in her suicide, leaving Anya an orphan. Back before she was Anya. When she was just Elaine Michaelson, just a girl with a family, with a father who made the wrong decisions and a mother too weak for this world. Rayna had preyed on the weakness of that family, and she had razed them all to hell.

And much like any revenge arc, Anya had needed both an in with the intended, and an accomplice to carry it out. Finding Teddy, hellbent on his revenge against the man who killed his father, was kismet, and everything that followed, the plan, the house, whispering in

Monomania

Rayna's ear, it had all gone flawlessly.

Anya had managed to manipulate not only the famous Ms. McCleod, but everyone who was working for her, had forced her way into the job, given away her best ideas and given Teddy the access he needed to seek his revenge.

And there was nothing to tie them to it. Nothing at all.

"How about we get a drink and celebrate?" she asks Teddy, shutting off the computer, leaving the edits for a time when she wasn't desperate to be in his presence.

"Let's do it," he replies, and leads her out the office by the hand.

All is well, that ends well.

Silently, in her head, Anya thanks Rayna for the promotion.

Elton Skelter

EPILOGUE

Behind the camera, the team silences the room, ensure the lights are focused just right. Makeup steps back after ensuring she's powdered just right, and Anya practices a smile that will light up the screen.

Who else would be better to tell this story? She had argued as such with the network when news of Rayna's unfortunate demise in the massacre had reached the station. She had been there from the get-go, and Rayna would have wanted her protégé to take control. It had barely been a challenge at all to get them to agree to it.

"Quiet on set," the director calls from the dark, and Anya takes a breath, faces the auto prompt, and fixes her face to show the somber tone of the report.

"And...action."

ANYA:

What started as a documented support of survivors of some of America's most violent mass-killings came to a head today, when 30-year-old Elliot Hardy, the final victim of the Phi Kappa Delta Frat House Massacre, took his life.

His reason?

From a suicide note obtained by the body of Hardy, it seems his reasoning was guilt. Guilt for the murders committed ten years ago in the very frat house we are about to see in this report, and the murders that were committed there again in a new spate of killings, documented on film. What you are about to see here is the final statements of all those who entered that house, and viewers are advised that this may be difficult to watch.

Thus, solving a ten-year-long mystery of what really happened on the night of July 26th, 2013.

This special is dedicated to our producer, Rayna McCleod, who lost her life in search of the story.

Anya smiles a shy smile at the camera, taking her place as the final replacement, taking Rayna's life yet again.

History is rewritten.

The story will be told…in her way.

END.

Monomania

Elton Skelter

www.ingramcontent.com/pod-product-compliance
Lightning Source LLC
LaVergne TN
LVHW021715060526
838200LV00050B/2677